Also by Angela McAllister

The Tide Turner
The Runaway

The Double Life of Cora Parry

The Double Life of Cora Parry

Angela McAllister

Orion
Children's Books

First published in Great Britain in 2011
by Orion Children's Books
a division of the Orion Publishing Group Ltd
Orion House
5 Upper St Martin's Lane
London WC2H 9EA
An Hachette UK company

1 3 5 7 9 10 8 6 4 2

A catalogue record for this book is
available from the British Library.

Trade paperback ISBN 978 1 84255 603 0
Hardback ISBN 978 1 4440 0151 8

Printed in Great Britain by CPI Mackays, Chatham ME5 8TD

The Orion Publishing Group's policy is to use papers that are natural, renewable
and recyclable products and made from wood grown in sustainable forests. The
logging and manufacturing processes are expected to conform to the environ-
mental regulations of the country of origin.

www.orionbooks.co.uk

*This book is dedicated to Mark and Sue,
with many thanks for their help, and to Jenny
for her invaluable insight and encouragement.*

❧ 1 ❧

Cora Parry stood in the lane, staring at the house she'd lived in for eleven years as if she'd never seen it before. To anyone passing, the neat cottage and tidy country garden appeared the same as usual, but for Cora everything was different today. Everything had changed for ever.

How often I've dreaded going home, she thought. How many times I've held back at this gate, scared of a beating for getting dirty in the woods or being late for a meal. Now the house was empty. There was no one watching at the window, waiting to grab her by the hair as she stepped inside. Martha Parry was dead and buried. She's gone, she's really gone and I'm free! Cora flung her arms wide and took a deep breath of the apple-sweet air. She felt as though a heavy winter shawl had fallen from her shoulders and let the gold September sun shine right into her heart and bones. *From this day I shan't answer to anyone. I'll be myself and do as I please.*

'Everything all right, Miss Carrie?'

She swung round. Old Ned the carter, who'd brought her back from the graveyard, had paused to light a pipe before his last mile home. He stared at her with a puzzled frown. Cora shrugged. *Why should I pretend?* she thought, leaning over the wall and snapping a fat red hip off the rose bush. *I'm happy and I don't care who knows it.*

'It was a shocking way to go,' Ned murmured. 'Nobody's been struck down by lightning on Furzy Heath in living memory.' He buttoned up his tobacco pouch and sucked thoughtfully on his pipe. 'Plenty of trees over the years, yes, well you'd expect that. But never a woman, leaving nothing to bury but a box of cinders. No, no. Not in living memory.' He crossed himself solemnly as a protection against the same fate. 'Best make yourself a cup of strong tea, Miss Carrie.'

'It's Cora. My name's Cora. Short for Victoria, like the Queen.'

Ned looked hurt. He turned away, muttering under his breath. Without another word he clicked his tongue and flicked the reins to tell his old horse to walk on.

Cora kicked the gatepost, cross with herself for being so sharp. After all, he'd only been breaking the awkward silence of their journey home. She knew he meant nothing by it, but that name, Carrie, seemed to haunt her and she hated it. Ever since Elijah Parry had adopted Cora from the workhouse when she was three years old and given her his surname, people often ran the two names together and called her Carrie. It's humiliating, she thought, as if who I am doesn't matter.

Cora had never really felt she knew who she was. Elijah had always treated her as a daughter but his wife, Martha, made it clear that she never thought of her as anything but a workhouse girl. 'You were born on the street,' she'd say. 'It's in your dirty blood.'

It might be of no consequence to Ned the carter, but that name was once all she'd owned in the world.

Cora sighed and let herself into the house. Alone at last, she untied the ribbon of her black bonnet and threw it on a chair. There had been talk of looking for Martha's will at the funeral, but Cora didn't want to do that now. She just wanted to enjoy these first hours of her new freedom without thinking about the future. Freedom, glorious, wonderful freedom. She gazed around the little hall. Everything felt strangely calm. Even the silence was different now, no longer tense with anticipation of Martha's brisk step.

Elijah's tall thumb stick caught her eye, still resting where he'd left it beside the door, although he'd been dead six years. She felt the polish of his fingers on its cleft handle, reminding her of their Sunday walks over the heath. Every few steps he would stop and crouch with her beside some tiny plant, or point at a bird in a tree, patiently teaching her the names of things: heather, magpie, yew. He'd made her chant the words over and over until they were planted in her mind. Elijah knew that names were important. When you call something by its name you bring it to life, he'd told her. You allow it to live in your mind.

How different Martha had been. There, beside his stick was her black cane. Instinctively, Cora rubbed her palms. *I won't take a beating with that again.* She took the cane, rested her foot on the edge of the chair and broke it across her knee with a satisfying snap. The pieces clattered to the floor. Even now Martha's words rang in her ears.

'What made him think I would want a girl in the house? Bringing you home, without word or warning – from the workhouse of all places!' Cora would listen, grinding the shame between her teeth. 'You may sit at his elbow with a book by the fire, girl, but in my kitchen you'll skivvy and make yourself useful – or else you'll go back, I warn you, quick as I can throw a scrubbing brush.'

When Elijah died, Cora had been terrified that Martha would send her back. But by then she'd come to rely on Cora's help in the house. Many times Cora wondered if the workhouse could really be worse than Martha's cold, cruel regime.

She stared into the hall mirror and tilted her chin imperiously. *I am mistress of the house now.* A girl with tumbling chestnut hair, moss-green eyes and high cheekbones sprinkled with freckles, stared back.

'That hair has far too much red in it for respectability,' she'd once heard Martha remark, archly. 'Gypsy eyes, not to be trusted.'

'But I am here and you are gone,' Cora whispered close

to the glass, not quite believing that Martha couldn't hear. Her face disappeared in a mist of breath. What would her future be? If only the mist would clear to reveal her fate in the glass.

Cora spent the afternoon opening drawers and cupboards, looking in all the places that had once been forbidden. She didn't notice the sky darken as she wrapped Martha's best plaid shawl around her shoulders. If I was a schoolmaster's wife I'd let all the village children play in my garden, she thought, admiring herself in a hand mirror. For Cora, whose imagination had been her only playmate growing up, it was a familiar game.

Before long wind and rain beat at the windows. She put everything back exactly in its place, feeling oddly guilty, and went downstairs to light the fire in the parlour.

That evening, a relentless gale racketed around the house. Cora investigated every cupboard and crock in the pantry, helping herself to whatever she wanted. It was the best supper she'd ever had – although she couldn't quite banish the feeling that Martha might walk into the kitchen at any moment and discover her feast. When she'd finished, feeling full and pleased with herself, she returned to the comfort of the parlour, kicked off her shoes and curled up on the armchair in front of the fire.

Cora's eyes rested on Elijah's favourite painting,

hanging above the mantelpiece. She'd always liked the colourful garden with its open gate, revealing a glimpse of sand dunes and sparkling sea beyond. The fact he'd found it in London the day he'd brought her home bound them together in her mind. But there was an unsettling feeling about it, as if something was missing – somebody. It seemed to invite you to step inside, to make the picture complete. Cora wondered whether Elijah had ever imagined walking into the picture, like she did. The thought made her smile. She shut her eyes and followed, trailing her fingers through the garden flowers, then barefoot on the warm sand, with the sea breeze in her hair.

Suddenly the front door was thrust open and someone crashed into the house out of the storm. Cora jumped up in alarm. Who would burst in without knocking? She ran to the hall in her stockinged feet but came to an abrupt stop.

A huge, bear-like figure filled the hallway. He looked up, stamping his muddy boots, and scowled angrily at Cora. His red face was framed by heavy black brows, windswept hair and a wild beard, dripping with rain. A flurry of wet leaves blew in around him through the open door. Cora's first thought was to reach for Elijah's stick, but it lay out of reach behind the stranger. She knew at once, from the grim set of his jaw as he slammed the door and heaved the heavy coat from his back, that his business would be bad for her.

'Keep out of my way, girl!' His black eyes flashed. 'You were no kin to my sister and you're no kin to me.'

Cora backed against the wall, shaking with fear. The stranger threw his coat on the chair and pushed past her towards the study. Martha had once spoken of a brother she had said was 'best forgotten'. What had she meant? Why was he here now?

Lowering his head to enter the study, Martha's brother made straight for Elijah's desk. Cora followed and watched, not daring to speak as he cast the chair aside and set about inspecting the contents of each drawer in turn. All she could do was watch with growing anger as he cast Elijah's treasured books and papers to the floor. After several minutes, not finding anything to interest him, he pulled a hip flask from his pocket and sank lumpenly into the chair. He unscrewed the lid and took a long draught of the liquor, which seemed to soothe him. Sighing deeply, he gestured to Cora to remove his boots.

Safest to do as he bid. She knelt before him, seething with fury at being treated like a servant. The filthy boots were difficult to grip and as each one came free in her hands she fell back, splattered with mud.

'Pack your things and make ready to leave before dawn,' he barked gruffly, as she got to her feet and brushed down her skirt.

'Where are you taking me?' She fought to control the emotion in her voice.

'You'll soon find out.'

'Will I be coming back?'

'No.'

'But this is my home!' She glared at him defiantly. 'You can't take me away.'

'Think yourself lucky I don't just throw you out, girl. You've no right to any of this now.'

Cora clenched her fists. How dare he come from

7

nowhere and tell her what to do! How dare he snatch away her new-found freedom and cast her out! Her eyes welled with tears but she was determined not to let him see them. She took a deep breath, gathered up her skirts, and walked slowly away.

As soon as she was out of his sight, Cora ran upstairs to her room and slammed the door. Her mind raced. She paced back and forth across the floor. *I won't go with him. I won't let him take me away. When he thinks I'm asleep I'll slip into Martha's bedroom and climb out of the window onto the roof of the lean-to. It should be easy to jump from there.* She'd almost tried it several times in the past but never dared, for fear of being locked in the woodshed if she was caught. But what then? Where could she go? She'd got no money, no friends. There wasn't anyone around here who'd take her in. Martha had seen to that.

Martha had always been afraid that Cora would talk about her in the village, so she'd lied to the other women, telling them Cora was wild and unmanageable, 'a deceitful little thief'. When Cora tried to make friends with the other girls she discovered they'd all been told to keep away from her. But Martha was the deceitful one. Cora knew right from wrong well enough, Elijah had taught her that. And she'd never stolen a thing in her life.

No, running away was a hopeless idea. Think calmly. She sat on the edge of the bed and took a deep breath to steady herself. Maybe it would be sensible to go with Martha's brother. And if things didn't look good wherever he took her, she could still run away if she had to.

Cora packed her few clothes and belongings into a

carpet bag and climbed into bed fully dressed, determined to be ready to face whatever was going to happen next. For a moment she was tempted to help herself to a pair of Martha's boots, but the idea of wearing them made her shudder. At least I'll be leaving everything that reminds me of her behind, she thought. But it was a relief mixed with regret. She'd be leaving all that reminded her of Elijah too. She couldn't go without something of his to take with her. All the books they'd read together were downstairs in the study, out of reach. There must be something else. Earlier that day she'd found six handkerchiefs in Martha's drawer, handkerchiefs that she'd embroidered for Elijah. Cora retrieved them, tucked them into her bag and then climbed back into bed.

She stared up into the darkness, wondering what was going to happen next. Elijah had once told her that she would only be happy if she learned to accept her lot. He'd said Martha was unhappy because she couldn't accept the fact she was unable to bear a child. Barren, he'd called it. Even the word sounded cold and miserable. Cora had often wondered whether Martha's cruelty towards her was some sort of punishment for not being her own daughter. Well, she thought, whatever the reason and whatever lies ahead, I won't just accept my lot. I won't let this man, or anyone, treat me like that again.

Cora lay, wide awake, listening to the stranger's lusty snoring in the parlour below. Head spinning, heart thumping, she waited for the footsteps on the stairs and the shout in the night.

❧ 2 ❧

A bang in the dark. Cora woke, drowsy and confused. Something was wrong. The collar of her dress was clenched tight in her fist, she felt the weight of boots on her feet. With a jolt she remembered the stranger downstairs.

Cora lugged the carpet bag awkwardly down the narrow stairs, feeling her way in the darkness. She heard the chink of the bread crock in the pantry then a glow of light bloomed in the passage below and Martha's brother emerged from the kitchen, carrying a candlestick. He stopped and stared up at her, his face eerily distorted by the flame. Cora lost her footing and stumbled down the last step.

When she looked up, he thrust out his hand, offering her a stale crust of bread.

'No,' she said, straightening her cloak. 'No, thank you.'

'Take it,' he muttered insistently. She stuffed the crust in the pocket of her skirt. It was a small kindness. Maybe things would turn out well after all.

Outside, a carriage waited in the rain, hunched like a monstrous black beetle; the coachman's wet leathers shone in the lamplight. Suddenly Cora wished they could have left during the day, to have one last glimpse of the only home she'd known. She covered her head with her hood and dashed out into the storm. At the carriage door she paused to glance back, but the candle was already snuffed out behind her and the dark, empty house had disappeared in the moonless night. The world was no more than a glittering splash of road, stamped by impatient hooves.

With a heavy heart, Cora climbed into the carriage and Martha's brother clambered in after her, tipping it violently as he arranged himself on the seat beside her. Without a word, he pulled his hat down and his collar up and turned his face to the shuttered window, sinking into some private brooding. Cora clasped her bag tight.

'Can you tell me where we're going?' she asked.

'Just sleep,' came the reply. 'You'll find out soon enough.'

Cora edged away from the smell of stale smoke and whisky that hung about him and drew her long, woollen cloak about her for warmth. With a clink of the harness the carriage lurched forward, and they clattered away into the night.

The carriage rocked along at an urgent pace, mile after mile, and before long the swaying motion and monotonous drumming of rain on the roof started to lull Cora to sleep. Each time she felt her eyes begin to close she roused herself, determined to stay awake. But the urge to sleep was strong, to sleep and escape the fear of not knowing what lay ahead. She stretched her legs as best she could in the tiny compartment and tried to think of something cheerful. Elijah's painting. She saw a room, bright with sunlight, gauzy curtains dancing at the open window and outside, a garden running down to the sea. In the room she imagined a little table with a jug of primroses and, beside the table, a plump bed with a sprigged quilt. On the bed lay a white dress, freshly laundered and trimmed with ribbon. Somehow she knew it would smell of lavender. Somehow she knew if she wore that dress she would never be afraid again. Cora looked at the dark figure hunched beside her. You can take away everything I have but you can't touch my dreams, she thought fiercely. Wherever I'm going, it will be a new start. I won't be the workhouse girl any more.

Eventually the pitch and roll of country lanes gave way to the fast toll road. Still the relentless rain teemed down, but now Cora heard other carriages thunder past and at last a dim sliver of dawn slipped under the shutters. She began to hear street sounds: wagons and carts rattling along the cobblestones; carters shouting to each other; horses whinnying to be home and dry. We must be in the city, she thought excitedly. London! She'd not been back here since Elijah took her away. This was where she'd been born, where she came from. Cora tried to reach forward and push the shutter aside to look out, but to her annoyance her companion slept with his legs jammed across her side of the compartment. Any movement would almost certainly wake him. She contented herself with listening keenly, imagining the scene outside.

Suddenly the coachman shouted, causing a commotion from the horses, and the carriage stopped abruptly. Cora's bag was flung from her arms onto the floor and Martha's brother woke with a jolt. He spat out an angry curse.

Cora picked up her bag. She felt bolder now with the city about her. 'Won't you tell me where we're going now? I have a right to know.'

He glowered darkly but didn't answer. Instead he poked the shutter catch with his cane and it rattled open.

Cora stared out through a veil of rain. They had stopped beside a pair of huge, forbidding gates. Beyond the gates was a gloomy courtyard streaming with water from overflowing gutters and flooded drains, surrounded on three sides by tall red brick buildings with ranks of barred windows. Arching over the entrance in large iron letters were the words: WALSTON WORKHOUSE.

Cora's blood ran cold. She sank back into her seat.

The man wrestled impatiently with the door and flung it open. 'Go on,' he barked loudly. 'This is where you came from.'

She stared at his clenched jaw and cold eyes in disbelief. 'You can't do this …' She was paralysed. Afraid to go but too frightened to refuse.

He raised his hand as if to strike her. 'Get out!' Cora snatched up her bag and scrambled down the carriage step. At once the door slammed shut. All her excitement at returning to London turned to terror. He was going to leave her alone in the city with nothing and nowhere to go but the one place she dreaded in the world. How stupid she'd been! Why had she thought he might take her anywhere else?

Even the grim coach seemed like a sanctuary now. Cora dropped her bag and gripped the rim of the carriage window, clinging to the narrow frame.

'You can't leave me here, Sir! Not here, please …' The horses stamped impatiently. She looked up at the coachman but he turned away.

The man leaned forward. 'I owe you nothing, girl,' he hissed. 'D'you hear?' He tipped his cane to rap her

14

knuckles. Cora flinched and drew them away. She heard him thump on the roof.

'Get going, man,' he shouted. 'And quick about it!'

The coachman cracked his whip and the horses pulled away. Cora darted clear of the carriage wheels but tripped backwards over her bag and lost her balance. She hit the ground hard and a sharp pain shot through her elbow.

Immediately city life was upon her, throngs of people hurrying past, heads down against the rain, pushing forward without paying her any heed. The street clamoured with traffic. A pair of coach horses in fine livery trotted towards her. Cora edged away from the roadside, tugging the hem of her cloak out of the gutter just in time. Glancing up as the coach passed she saw a face at the window: the face of a girl her own age, with green eyes and thick curls of chestnut hair, framed by a velvet collar and hat. Their eyes met for a fraction of a second. Two worlds, two fates, momentarily collided. Then the wheels spun past, splashing through a deep rut in the road and drenching Cora with cold, dirty water.

Cora sat on the pavement, shaken and shamed. As the water soaked through her clothes a hot anger began to burn in her blood. Anger at Martha's brother, anger at herself for not running away the night before, anger at the world for not caring, for casting her into the gutter outside the workhouse gate.

She gathered up the things that had spilled from her bag, stuffed them back inside and staggered to her feet.

Cora brushed the dripping hair from her face and stood defiantly before Walston's iron arch. Martha had always called it the last resort of the desperate and mad. 'Be grateful for what you've got here,' she'd warned as she'd served Cora a meagre supper of bread and dripping. 'The gruel's so thin in that place that inmates pick raw meat from marrow bones. Some are so starved that they scavenge peelings left for the pigs.'

Cora had learned not to listen, learned to protect herself. Her mind had buried any painful memories of the workhouse in its deepest recesses long ago. All memories of her mother were buried with them. Although Cora tried to recall her mother's face and hear her voice, she had never been able to conjure it from the darkness. The past evaded her like a forgotten dream.

But now here it was. Cold, hard and real. It was as if she'd woken up to discover that all her years at the schoolmaster's cottage had been the dream. This nightmare was her new reality. *My mother must have stood right here with me in her arms, sick and penniless with nowhere else to go.* Cora knew at once she would rather die than step through those gates.

 3

ora turned her back on the workhouse and walked away. She allowed herself to be jostled along the street until she came to the steps of a Temperance Hall. She pushed her way out of the crowd and sat against a pillar, shivering in her damp clothes.

So, this is the city. Cora had been born here, but now it was a foreign world to her. Filth, noise, the foul stink of sewers. Acrid smoke belched from a forest of chimneys as people emerged from soot-blackened houses and shops; tradesmen propped open their shutters and gangs of barefoot children played in the street; pedlars and tinkers followed their donkey-barrows; a pair of flower sellers clutched their skirts as they sidestepped to avoid the open drains and piles of dung smeared all over the road; delivery boys darted left and right to dodge a drenching from the drays and trolleys that splashed through the puddles.

There isn't a soul in this city who cares if you live or die, Cora Parry, she told herself. You've got to rely on your instincts now – after all, this is where you came from. She heard Martha's scornful words. 'The street is in your dirty blood.' She'd have to hope it was true.

Realising that the rain had stopped at last, Cora pushed back her hood and shook the drips from her hair. She noticed a rough-looking boy with a black eye, slouching in a doorway across the street, stroking a cat in his arms. He was the only person who didn't seem preoccupied with the business of the day. Everyone else has somewhere to go or something to do. They don't even see me, she thought bitterly.

She was distracted from her thoughts by a coffee vendor setting up her stall across the road. The old woman polished a cup with her dirty apron and tasted her first brew. Satisfied to the last drop, she dried her lips with the back of her mittened hand and started to call out her wares.

'Ha'penny coffee! Steaming hot!' Soon she was doing brisk business. Beside her another barrow was piled high with bread rolls. Its red-faced proprietor fried bacon on a brazier, grinning cheerfully as the irresistible smell brought customers swarming round. Suddenly Cora remembered the crust Martha's brother had given her. She thrust her hand into her pocket and felt what was now a soggy lump. Her heart sank, but she pulled it out and ate it all the same. The bacon man watched her as he flipped the spitting rashers. When she caught his eye he whistled and beckoned her over.

Cora couldn't believe her luck. She hurried across the road, darting between the carts and carriages. 'This'll warm you up,' he said and offered her a greasy paper parcel.

She hesitated. 'I can't pay.'

The bacon man stuffed the parcel into her hands. 'Take it and scram,' he said, 'or I'll have every waif and stray at my elbow.' He turned back to his spitting pan and she took a chance to snatch a moment in the brazier's warmth before making her way back across the road.

Inside the parcel was a tangle of crisp bacon rinds, an overcooked rasher and a small roll. Cora lifted the golden rind to her mouth, savouring the salty smell. But before she could eat it a huge dog snatched the rind from her fingers, then thrust its head and paws into her lap and devoured the parcel, strewing shreds of paper everywhere.

'Get off, brute!' She jumped up and beat it away, but too late; every lick of bacon was gone and the loaf trodden into dirty crumbs on the pavement. Cora picked up a stone and threw it after the dog in frustration.

She was brushing the greasy crumbs from her cloak when somebody grabbed her by the arm from behind and swung her round.

'I've been watching you!' A bearded man with bloodshot eyes and broken teeth grinned in her face. Cora tried to push him away but he gripped her tight.

'Let go! What do you want? Let me go!' She tried to

pummel his chest with her fists. To her horror, he clasped her wrists and shackled them with one huge hand.

'You ain't got nowhere to go, 'ave you?' He nodded in the direction of the workhouse. 'You don't want to be going in there, girl. Nasty things happen to girls like you in there. Come with me.' The man locked both arms around her. Cora opened her mouth to scream. He slapped a filthy hand across her face.

'Hush now. I ain't gonna do you no harm. I'm here to help you. I'll give you work.' She twisted away from his stinking breath. 'I'll look after you, girl.' Cora lunged forward and bit his hand.

'That's not friendly!' he snarled. Clamping her close to his chest, he began to haul her along the street.

Then, out of nowhere, a boy ran up and kicked him hard in the shins. The man let out a fierce curse and groaned with pain. He released Cora and clutched his legs. Before she could understand what was happening the boy had grabbed her hand and she found herself being dragged away down a side street, into a maze of dark alleys.

4

Cora clung tight and ran, dodging and swerving behind the boy, grateful to be saved. When they reached the entrance to a narrow passage he paused to glance back over his shoulder and pulled Cora inside, pushing her into a dark doorway and wedging himself in beside her. She felt her carpet bag slam against her knee – he must have grabbed it with his other hand. Cora's heart was thudding so fast she thought it would burst. Crushed against the boy's shoulder, she noticed he was older than she was, a head taller and thick-set, with a strong feral smell, like the trace of fox.

For a moment they both held their breath and listened for footsteps. Cora's head throbbed. She felt sick with fright.

'We weren't followed,' the boy murmured. 'The kidsman was just taking a chance.'

He waited a moment longer then led her out into the street once more.

'Thank you.' Cora sighed with relief and rubbed her sore wrists. 'Who was that man? Do you know him?'

'Everyone round here knows him,' said the boy. 'He runs gangs of kids on the streets – picks up strays and orphans and sets them to work, then leeches off them.' Cora shuddered. She could still smell his repulsive stench on her. As she straightened her twisted sleeves the boy leaned against a lamppost and looked her up and down.

'I saw you thrown out of that carriage this morning.'

Cora looked at him in surprise. Now she could see his face properly she recognised the boy who'd been stroking the cat. The kidsman hadn't been the only one watching her. It seemed she wasn't so invisible after all.

'I've got nowhere to go,' she said simply. Her whole existence was reduced to this one fact.

'No family?'

Cora shook her head. The boy seemed interested and eyed her more intently. At once she wished she hadn't given so much away. 'But I can look after myself now,' she added. He just grinned.

There was something about him that puzzled her. Something furtive about the way he sunk his head between his shoulders and pulled the peak of his grubby cap low across his forehead. He looked older than she was, but his voice sounded young. His jacket was too tight, pinched around his shoulders and short in the arms, but his trousers were too big, tied at the waist with a leather belt, turned-up at the bottom and worn through from scuffing on the ground. His nails and hair were dirty but his eyes were bright, keen as a buzzard. He looked as though he'd just taken a beating but he stared boldly at her as if she was for sale in a shop window.

'It's a shiner, eh?' Cora realised that she'd been staring. 'A lamppost done it – just jumped out at me.' She shuffled her feet, not sure what to say.

'How old are you?' he asked bluntly.

'Fourteen.'

'Tiny, ain't yer? Like a little bird.' It was true, but Cora didn't like being reminded of it. She knew she was small for her age, half-starved from the years of Martha's mean rations. The boy reached out, took both her hands in his and turned them over. 'Little hands.'

'They're strong!' she retorted, pulling them away. She was beginning to dislike this boy, even if he *had* saved her from trouble.

'Not strong enough to fight off the kidsman.' He pulled a liquorice stick out of his pocket and offered it to her. 'Come on, then, Bird. I'll look after you. I know somewhere you can stay.'

Cora hesitated. 'What sort of place?' She couldn't resist the liquorice.

He smiled. 'A rookery – just the place for a little bird to nest. What's your name?'

'Cora.' She thrust her chin in the air and gave him a

look that said, 'you'd do well to remember it'. 'And I'm strong as any boy,' she added.

He smirked with approval and kicked a stone at an apple core in the road. The stone hit its target and the core spun and bounced out of sight into the gutter. Cora watched. There was something edgy, intense about him, that made her wary. But what else was she going to do? Go on wandering the streets? Or worse, go back to Walston? That decided it. 'What's your name, then?'

'Fletch, they call me.' He stared meaningfully, holding her with his gaze as if waiting for her to notice something left unsaid.

Cora suddenly understood what had been confusing her: the voice, the soft features beneath the mask of dirt and bruised skin and the odd fit of the clothes. 'You're a girl!' She felt her cheeks flush.

'Sharp, ain't you!' Fletch laughed, enjoying Cora's embarrassment.

Cora frowned, annoyed. 'Why did you let me ...'

'That's all right. It suits me, being taken for a boy.' A bell rang out nearby. 'Are you hungry?' Cora nodded.

'Come on, then.' Fletch walked off, heading towards the street corner, where a man with a tray of cakes hanging from his neck was ringing out his wares. Relieved to discover that her strange new friend was a girl, Cora followed. At least she'd be safe with a girl.

'Sweet an' spicy ginger!'

Fletch bought them each a chunk of gingerbread, insisting on the biggest for her money and crammed the cake into her mouth as if she hadn't eaten in a week. Cora remembered the dog that had stolen her bacon and held her own cake close. 'Thanks,' she said. 'I'll pay you back.'

'Come on, then, follow me,' said Fletch, licking her fingers, and she started off at a pace.

Cora followed, eating her cake as best as she could, as they hurried through a labyrinth of squalid streets. What sort of place is she taking me to, she wondered, running to keep up. And why would a girl want to disguise herself as a boy? It was no use trying to question Fletch as they pushed their way through a multitude of people growing noisier and more numerous with every turn. Cora was amazed by the sea of faces; she had no idea there were so many people in the city. There was an urgency, an energy about everyone – the street cries, the bargaining, arguing, shouting. Every push and shove felt as though it was rubbing away her sleepy country life, every step taking her into an exciting, unpredictable new world.

Something hard crashed into Cora's feet, almost knocking her over. A boy with stump legs sitting on a trolley had wheeled himself into Cora's path. He thrust his arm out towards her and rattled a coin in a sardine tin.

'Give us a penny, Miss. Have pity, Miss.'

Cora rubbed her ankle. 'I don't have one,' she said impatiently, worried she might lose sight of Fletch, but he stared up at her with pleading eyes and shook the tin hard. Cora saw the bloodstains on the grubby bandages wrapped around his stumps and felt ashamed that she'd snapped at him. The boy fixed his eyes on the remains of her gingerbread. Cora sighed and dropped it into his outstretched hand. 'It's all I have, really,' she said, watching him devour the cake in one mouthful. With a nod of thanks he took up his tin-rattling again and she hurried on.

Meanwhile Fletch was weaving further ahead, almost invisible in the crowd. Cora pushed her way through, ducking to avoid slops splashing down from a window above, only to collide with a bird seller loaded with cages. She scrambled away from the explosion of screeching finches just in time to catch sight of Fletch turning right into a passage ahead.

She reached the passage, hot and breathless, and came to an abrupt halt. Where had Fletch gone? Cora took a deep breath and stepped inside. After twenty slow paces stumbling over litter and broken bottles, she was relieved to see a faint light ahead, revealing a sharp turn left. Fletch had not vanished – just disappeared out of sight. Cora turned the corner and saw an archway, and beyond that a glimpse of dilapidated buildings and children playing leapfrog in a dirty courtyard.

At the end of the passage she caught up with Fletch, who was bent over an old man sitting on a wooden tub. A painted sign on the wall behind him said 'Farthing Court'.

Cora gazed, wide-eyed at the scene. Farthing Court was a slum of tall, ruinous houses, with peeling plaster and weeds sprouting from their damp, sagging walls, all clustered around a cobbled square scattered with ragged children and a menagerie of animals. Women perched and preened at open windows, leaning on their elbows, chattering and calling to each other above the noise of babies crying within. Some spoke in foreign accents Cora couldn't understand and their shrill voices echoed around the yard like a flock of birds in the trees. She could see why Fletch called it a rookery.

The old man had pulled Fletch close. Cora guessed from his tattered breeches that he must have been a sailor long ago, but now he wore a woman's shawl over his jacket and patches on both his eyes.

'Can you 'ear it, Fletch ...' he wheezed. 'Can you 'ear the sea?'

'The tide's coming in, Nelson,' Fletch replied, '... white horses an' all.' She tugged her arm away. 'Let us go then, eh? I'll bring you shrimps tomorrow, I promise.'

'You take care of old Nelson,' he muttered, releasing her with a nod. 'Keep them gulls away.' He waved his bony hands about his head. 'Keep 'em away.'

Cora looked up for the gulls, but only pigeons sat on the grey washing hanging from poles above their heads.

Fletch took Cora by the elbow. 'Stick with me,' she said. 'Do as I say here and you'll be all right.'

Cora was alarmed by her change in tone. Why would she need her protection? What sort of people lived here?

At the far end of the courtyard she noticed a tavern, The Hole in The Wall. A huddle of men played cards at a table outside, an assortment of mangy dogs slouched at their feet. As Cora followed Fletch across the yard a sudden disagreement flared up between two of the men, setting the dogs barking at each other. At the same moment a tribe of barefoot boys burst through the passage and ran into the yard, chased by a gang throwing stones. As soon as the gang saw the dogs they took fright, turned tail and ran straight out again. The boys sent them packing with loud jeers and whistles, hopping from foot to foot, triumphantly. At this, the women laughed and the men forgot their argument and joined in. Cora couldn't help but smile. She'd never seen such an extraordinary collection of people. The feeling of community in the court made Cora wish she belonged somewhere.

'Don't be taken in,' said Fletch, under her breath. She steered Cora firmly away. 'Most of them would turn nasty if you crossed them. And the women are the worst.'

Unnerved, Cora walked on with her eyes to the ground. This place, this girl. Nothing was as it seemed. What was she getting into?

They crossed the court towards a boarded-up house in the opposite corner of the yard. Its four storeys seemed about to topple over each other like badly stacked bricks. Fletch didn't go to the front door but descended some steps to an entrance below street level.

Cora hesitated at the top and stared down into the dark, damp stairwell. Fletch swung round with her hand on the door below.

'You coming?'

Cora looked back over her shoulder. The streets weren't safe, where else could she go? With a nervous nod, she followed Fletch below.

✺ 5 ✺

It took a moment for Cora's eyes to adjust to the dimness of the cellar. The only light came from a broken window by the door that was patched with brown paper, suffusing the room with a dingy glow, but it didn't reach the back of the chamber, which disappeared in darkness. The damp air smelled of mould and unwashed bodies and the floor was strewn with rubbish – old sacks, boxes and bundles of rags. Cora felt as though she had entered the lair of some burrowing beast.

As she stared, shadows began to stir and figures emerged from the heaps of rags. Pale faces peered out of the darkness. Was it possible that people actually lived here? Now Cora saw a sick-looking man covered with a pile of potato sacks. A broken basket rustled as a baby stirred inside. Lying beside the basket was a woman who began to cough feebly, barely flinching as a rat scurried over the hem of her skirt and away across the earthen floor. Their wretchedness seeped into Cora like a chill.

'You can sleep there,' said Fletch, pointing to a stained mattress lying on the floor against the wall, beneath a broken shelf. 'It's my patch.' Cora looked at the bed with disgust, certain it was riddled with lice.

'If anyone asks, say I brought you here. They won't give you any bother.' Fletch turned to leave.

'Where are you going,' asked Cora uneasily.

'That'll be my business,' said Fletch. 'Stay here. I'll be back.' Cora couldn't see Fletch's face in the shadow but she heard the warning in her voice. Don't ask questions.

Cora sat gingerly on Fletch's mattress and pulled her damp cloak around her. How had everything changed so quickly? Cora thought back over the two weeks since Martha's accident, the shock in the village and her hasty, grim funeral. She realised now she'd been stupid to think her life would be better just because Martha was gone. She'd really imagined she'd be able to do as she pleased. *How many times did Martha tell me I had no right to expect anything, and that I'd end up back where I came from?* Cora looked around the miserable cellar. The thought of Martha being right was infuriating.

She opened the carpetbag and took out a tiny rag doll, no bigger than her hand, the doll she had carried the day she entered the workhouse. Belle, her silent companion, had shared every childhood secret, every tear. She fingered the doll's woollen plaits. We've got to watch and learn like we did before, when Elijah brought us home, Belle, she said silently. We've got to learn how to get by on the streets now, like this girl Fletch.

Cora stared into the gloom, overcome with tiredness. She looked about for a blanket. Stuffed down between the mattress and the wall was a tobacco tin containing a few candle stubs, two chipped tankards and an assortment of bundles of various sizes wrapped in rag and string. There were no blankets, only an old military greatcoat without any buttons and a few more sacks. Cora made a rough pillow of the sacks and pulled the coat over herself, exhausted. Although it was the middle of the afternoon, within minutes she was asleep.

She woke several hours later to the rattle of a heavy object being dragged down the cellar steps. For a moment Cora couldn't remember where she was, but the smell soon reminded her. It was dark outside now and the lights of braziers in the courtyard flickered like fireflies at the papered window. A silhouette stumbled through the door. Fletch?

The heavy object banged against something and a boy cursed, waking the baby who began to cry.

'Shush now, shush.' A young mother's voice in the darkness, the sound of her reaching across the creaking basket, then the thirsty gasps of the baby being suckled.

Cora sat up, pulled her bag close and nestled against the wall, listening to the woman's whispers. Hunger gnawed at her stomach and her elbow throbbed where she'd fallen on the pavement earlier that day. I'm not going to just sit here and wait for Fletch, she thought. She would get up and find something to eat herself. Just then, there were footsteps on the stairs. The windows glowed brightly, the door opened and lantern light flooded the room, revealing a man in a patched scarlet waistcoat and a battered top hat.

'I tell you all me money was stolen, right out of this very pocket,' he blustered to a woman who followed along behind. He picked his way unsteadily between the crates and boxes on the floor. 'It must have been a master cutpurse, the best in the city, to fleece Mordecai Beam.'

The lantern swayed, casting a warm light across the room and throwing shadows up the walls. The woman urged him on, towards the back of the room. 'And I say you drank every penny, Mr Beam. While your poor wife has been traipsing after that rag man all day, lame as a three-legged-dog, with nothing but bones worth taking in the rain this morning and all for fourpence ...'

Two boys arrived, squabbling together as one struggled with a sandwich board that advertised 'Mordecai Beam. Master of Mystification and Magic', while the other tried to push past impatiently.

'I sat at my cups, resisting temptation from dawn 'til ducks, I mean dusk, Mrs Beam,' insisted her husband with a hiccup. 'It was a fine show. The Punch and Judy professor finally took a chance, thought he could outwit the painted lady, but I had his money.'

'Then where is it now, Pa?' asked one of the boys cheekily. Mr Beam tried to cuff his son's ear but overbalanced and sat, with a thud, on an orange box.

The arrival of the Beam family brought life and colour to the cellar. They proceeded to occupy the whole width of the far end of the room, which was partly curtained off. Boxes and crates that had seemed rubbish in the shadows were deftly upended, spread with a cloth, which Mrs Beam fetched from behind the curtain, and served as makeshift table and chairs. The boys lit a couple of candles in jam jars and the scene became almost cosy.

Cora studied the rest of the room. A haunted-looking boy with a violent twitch was hunched in one corner, and beside him slumped a thin dog, scratching its fleas. He pulled a candle stub out of his pocket and went over to Mrs Beam to light it. A man with mournful eyes sat against a bolted door. Cora noticed his hands tremble as he unwrapped a cigar butt from a pile in his lap and shook out its contents into a tin. In another corner, a man and his wife, dressed all in black, huddled together rocking two small children in their arms. The twitching boy brought his light to their lantern and, without a word, the tiny comfort was shared.

Cora was surprised to see a face she recognised. The boy who had almost knocked her over with his trolley was now tucking into a meat pie. Gone were the pitiful stumps, miraculously replaced with a pair of sturdy legs. The red-stained bandages hung out of his pocket and the trolley, which she guessed was what had woken her up as it was dragged down the steps, now leaned against the wall. I gave him my cake, she thought, with annoyance.

Cora was distracted by a scraping sound on the steps outside. A stout woman, carrying half a dozen bags stuffed to bursting, pushed her way inside. She waddled painfully across the room on fat, bandaged feet, and came to sit near Cora. Cora couldn't help recoiling at her strong smell of stale sweat and edged away a little, but the woman took no notice. With much puffing and panting, she arranged her bags around herself, shifting them about as if they were fidgety children. Once settled, she pulled a plug of tobacco from her apron pocket, broke off a piece and sat, chewing it contentedly.

The youngest Beam boy came over and squatted beside one of the bags. He started to poke about inside.

'Find any treasure today, Marnie?' he asked mischievously.

Marnie smiled with blackened teeth then reached forward and pushed him sharply away. The boy fell back and knocked his head on an orange box, but scrambled off with a grin.

'Lots of treasure,' muttered Marnie, tugging the bags closer and shutting her eyes. 'Lots of lovely treasure to sell … silver bells and cockleshells. Buy me a crown, dearie. Who'll buy Queen Marnie a crown?'

Cora leaned towards her to peek at the treasure, but

there was nothing precious sparkling inside the bags – they were only filled with twigs and leaves, scraps of paper and dry nuggets of dung.

Cora moved discreetly away. She began to hope that Fletch would return soon.

The boy returned to his mother, rubbing his head. He looked back over his shoulder at Cora. 'There's a girl on Fletch's patch,' he said loudly.

Cora felt all eyes in the room upon her. She backed against the wall, wishing she could disappear into the shadows.

'Fletch... Fletch brought me here,' Cora stuttered. She glanced towards the door, measuring the distance. Should she run for it? But, as Fletch had promised, when they heard this, everyone turned back to their own business. The boy shrugged.

Mrs Beam studied Cora as she pinned a second shawl tightly over the one she already wore. 'Well,' she said with a smile. 'The poor girl can't have anywhere better to go if Fletch has brought her here, so that makes her one of us.' She turned her attention to her husband. 'Now, Mr Beam, you burp Nellie's baby. Do it good and proper, mind. Two burps. Don't stop 'til you've brought up two – one for the purpose and one for luck.'

'Luck! Dear Lady,' sighed Mr Beam. 'If only it could be had so easily.' Cora watched him approach the waif-like mother and baby. He stooped down and took the tiny child from her arms and rested it gently over his shoulder, then began to rock it, patting its back and humming a meandering tune, deep and growly in his chest.

Mrs Beam noticed Cora watching. 'He's a natural,' she said proudly. 'It's the spirit on 'is breath what really soothes them, but it keeps everyone happy.'

Cora smiled back. It was a strange world where anyone could talk of happiness in such circumstances. *Watch and learn.*

A shadow appeared in the doorway. Cora felt the mood in the room change, as if a cold wind had blown in, and most of the candles were hurriedly snuffed out. Mrs Beam took the baby from her husband's arms, laid it in its mother's lap and fussed Mr Beam away behind the curtain, beckoning to her boys to follow. There was a low growl from the dog and then a whine as it was smacked smartly across the nose. Fletch paused at the threshold, filling the doorway with her large frame. She scanned the interior with narrowed eyes.

There was something proprietorial about the way she surveyed the room, as though she owned it. What power did this girl who behaved like a boy have in this place?

Seeming satisfied that all was as it should be, Fletch stepped inside. As she crossed the room she pulled a package wrapped in newspaper from her jacket pocket and tossed it towards the man with the cigar butts. He deftly caught it and tipped his hat in thanks. Fletch sat down beside Cora and pulled another from her pocket.

'Supper, Marnie.' She unwrapped the bundle to reveal three piping hot potatoes inside. Marnie pushed her bags away and shuffled up close, grabbing a potato out of Fletch's hands like a rude, hungry child. Fletch handed the third to Cora.

Cora cradled the delicious warmth in her hands. 'Thank you.' She was grateful but she felt uneasy about taking more from Fletch. 'I'll pay you back, I promise. And for the cake.'

Fletch tore open her potato without taking her eyes off Cora. 'We'll find a way,' she replied.

I'll get some money tomorrow, thought Cora, pulling apart the papery skin and burning her fingertips as the steam escaped. From the reactions of the others, she knew she was right to be wary of Fletch. She didn't want to be in her debt a moment longer than necessary. While they ate, Cora watched the cigar man, who had taken his parcel over to the invalid lying in the corner of the room.

'Supper, Signor Peretti,' he said, sitting beside him and gently raising the man's stiff body in his arms. Signor Peretti looked up at him and smiled weakly. The man took off his own coat and wrapped it around the invalid's shoulders then he pulled a fork out of his waistcoat pocket and patiently proceeded to feed him small portions of potato.

Cora was moved by the way the people in the cellar looked after each other. They were almost like a family. But somehow Fletch didn't fit in. There was a dejected air about the rest of them. Fletch was strong and sure of herself.

Fletch wiped her mouth with her sleeve, screwed up the greasy newspaper and tossed it into a tea chest nearby. Her huge shadow loomed across the wall. Cora wondered how long she'd lived there, but Fletch had already made it plain that she didn't like questions, so she kept quiet.

Fletch sat back, pulled off her cap and ran her fingers through her short, thick hair. She began to untie her boots. 'While you're here: there's three rules, Bird, one, nobody touches anybody else's stuff; two, if you've got more than you need you share it out; and three, never, ever bring strangers here, or tell anyone about this place. Got it?'

Cora nodded. 'But you brought me?'

Fletch kicked one boot off, then the other. 'I make the rules.' She smiled at Cora with her mouth but not her eyes.

No wonder the other inhabitants seemed afraid of her. Cora picked up the boots and handed them to Fletch.

'Thank you for saving me today,' she mumbled, 'for bringing me here. I won't cause any trouble.'

'Just watch the others and you'll soon learn.' Fletch rummaged in the gap between the mattress and the wall and produced a battered tankard which she offered to Cora. 'You'll need this. There's a water pump in the court, or Bess'll fill it at the Hole tomorrow.' The tankard was too big to put in Cora's bag so she looked around for somewhere to hide it and decided to stow it in the tea chest.

Fletch yawned. 'Shove up, then.' She rolled up a hessian sack for her pillow and pummelled the mattress a few times with her fists. 'Have that side until you get a bed of your own.'

Cora shuffled across, took off her boots and lay down beside Fletch. Although her narrow portion of mattress was barely wide enough, she was too afraid to move to make herself more comfortable. Fletch lay, silent and still with her back to Cora. 'Fletch,' Cora said tentatively. 'How do people here get by?'

Fletch sighed and pulled the greatcoat over her shoulders. 'Rookin,' she muttered.

The cigar man snuffed out the last remaining candle. Now only lights from the yard glowed at the window.

'What's rookin'?' whispered Cora.

'You'll find out.'

6

When Cora woke late next morning, Fletch and most of the other inhabitants of the room had gone. Only the invalid, Signor Peretti, and the young mother remained. Cora stretched and yawned, wondering how she had slept so deeply that she hadn't heard the others leave. She gazed around the cellar in the hazy light. All evidence of the night's occupation had been artfully hidden away among the rubbish. There wasn't a tin cup or a candle stub to be seen. Apart from the two vagrant figures, nobody casting their eye in at the door would ever guess it was home to anyone except rats and mice. Even the baby had been tucked into its mother's rags.

Cora took a comb from her bag, untangled her hair and

twisted it into a bun. I've slept in this hole but I don't need to look like a tramp, she thought to herself. She pinned up her stray locks and wondered what to do next. *One thing I know, I'm not going to wait around here. I won't rely on Fletch's charity again.*

A rustle on the steps interrupted her thoughts. It was Mrs Beam returning with one of the boys, who was groaning miserably.

'Alfie, I swear I'll pull it out myself if you don't shut up,' she snapped, pushing him on before her. The boy clutched his jaw, his dirty face streaked with tears.

'Toothache,' Mrs Beam explained to Cora across the room. 'I've been all over for cloves but they don't seem to help him. Reckon it'll have to come out but I haven't got the money for extraction. He'll have to hope the sun shines on his father.'

Cora felt sorry for Alfie, no longer the mischief-maker of the night before but now a sorrowful figure who collapsed onto a mess of grubby blankets and sobbed like a baby. Mrs Beam produced a half-empty bottle from the dark depths of the room and took a twist of paper out of her pocket. She opened the paper and tipped some powder inside. Giving it a shake she took it over to the baby's mother.

'There's your medicine, Nellie, dear,' she said, exchanging the bottle for the baby. 'Fletch gave me the money for it.' Nellie thanked her and sipped it slowly.

Cora had never seen such a young baby. Mrs Beam noticed her watching and beckoned her over. Cora's curiosity overcame her shyness and she got up and went over to kneel beside them.

'Go on, hold his little hand,' said Mrs Beam. Cora stroked the baby's hand and its tiny fingers curled around her own. He seemed such a fragile creature, too pink and soft to exist in this filthy rat-infested place.

'What's your name, girl?' asked Mrs Beam, gently rocking the baby. 'Where did you come from?'

Cora liked Mrs Beam and her no-nonsense motherly way, but suddenly her past seemed precious and private.

'I'm an orphan,' she said.

'So you are one of us.' Mrs Beam laid the baby in the basket then made Nellie comfortable, arranging her tattered blankets.

'I don't know who I am,' said Cora truthfully. 'I've always made up stories about where I came from and who my parents might have been.'

'We all tell ourselves stories to get by,' said Mrs Beam with a wistful smile. 'Mordecai's story has a happy end where he buys the family another caravan and takes us on the road again.'

But I don't know what my story is, thought Cora. She looked at the dismal scene around her. 'I just need to learn to survive in the city,' she said. 'Like Fletch.'

'Fletch is a survivor, sure enough,' said Mrs Beam. 'She'll teach you all the tricks. But take my advice, girl, never cross her – she's got a temper like a wildcat. And she's dangerous too. Most of them in here work for her, but they're afraid of her.' Mrs Beam looked over at Alfie, clutching his jaw. 'Both my boys have got on the wrong side of Fletch and regretted it. Still, we're all grateful that she protects this place from trouble. Last winter she saw off two men who wanted to move in, real villains they was. Goodness knows what scum they'd have brought with them. They taunted Marnie, that's what made her mad.'

'What did she do?' Cora was alarmed to hear the truth about her bedfellow.

Mrs Beam turned her back on Alfie and lowered her voice. 'She told them if they wanted to take over they'd have to kill her first or they'd never sleep easy – 'cos she'd slit their throats in the night.' Cora shuddered.

'Something angry burns inside that girl,' said Mrs Beam. 'They scarpered when she threatened them with a knife in each hand. She's quick with a blade.'

Cora remembered what Fletch had said about women being the worst when they were crossed.

'Why does she do it – live here like this?'

'Why does anyone? But it's different for Fletch. This is her little kingdom,' said Mrs Beam. 'These slums are heaving with people like us, scavenging a living however we can. But Fletch wants to be better than that. She's important here, caring for the sick ones and the simple ones, like old Marnie. We all rely on her, one way or another. It looks like you need her too.'

Cora was starting to feel uneasy about her debt to Fletch. 'I can look after myself,' she insisted. 'I don't need anyone.'

Mrs Beam gave her a disapproving look. 'It'd be a lonely world if we all thought like that, dear,' she said. 'We look out for each other round here. You'll soon see that's how it works.'

Cora was cross with herself. Mrs Beam could see she was a scared, country girl who wouldn't last a day on the street. Even so, maybe she could help. She was much easier to talk to than Fletch.

'What's rookin'?' asked Cora.

Mrs Beam looked surprised. 'Rookin', well that's gambling,' she said. 'Swindling, mostly.'

'Is that how everyone here gets by?'

'Some have the nerve for it but it's a dangerous business in this neighbourhood,' said Mrs Beam with a sigh. 'The rest manage by their wit and whiskers. Folks seem willing to give Mr Beam their money all right and most days I can earn the extra by working for the rag 'n' bone, unless I'm called away for a toothache!' She nodded towards Alfie who was now being distracted from his pain by a brown mouse. 'My boys help the costers load up vegetables early at the market and then get delivery work if they're lucky. Mr Grindle, who sleeps by the boarded-up door over there, he's a long song seller and Jack Mint, the boy with the twitch, well, he's a dog stealer what dopes them and hides them away and usually gets a fine price for returning them a few days later.'

'Who are the family in black?' asked Cora.

'They're Russians,' said Mrs Beam. 'Fletch let them in because she could see they wouldn't cause any trouble. I don't expect they'll stay long. Their sort don't. They usually find their own kind after a while.'

Cora liked the idea of being able to find your own kind. It sounded like a happy end.

'Well, you've got us now,' said Mrs Beam, as if she'd guessed what Cora was thinking. 'You'll soon find your feet around here.'

'Would you help me, then?' asked Cora. 'Help me find work like the others?'

'Oh, well now ...' Mrs Beam suddenly looked flustered. 'That ain't something I can do – it ain't my business, see. Fletch brought you here, she'll fix you up, I'm sure.' Cora sighed. Was Fletch in charge of everything? Mrs Beam looked sorry for her. 'I suppose there's no harm in helping yourself, in the meantime,' she said, 'seeing as Fletch ain't around. You've got a fine bag over there – you'd get a good price if you pawned it.'

'Oh no, I can't part with that,' said Cora. The bag contained everything she owned, all that reminded her of her old life, no matter how unhappy.

'Well then, surely you've got something inside that you don't need? Mr Tally, the pawnbroker, will give tuppence for a good handkerchief. You'd dine like a princess on pea soup and eels for that.'

Cora looked across at the bag thoughtfully. Had she been too hasty? Here was a way to help herself. Maybe there was something she could do without.

Cora fetched her bag and rummaged inside. There were Elijah's six handkerchiefs. If she kept her favourite maybe she could part with the rest. She showed them to Mrs Beam.

'Oh yes, they'll fetch something,' said Mrs Beam, admiring her needlework. 'Take them round to Mite Street. It ain't far. Speak to old Mr Tally, he's kind to our sort. But don't have any business with the young one, Snub – he's got a heart of stone.'

Cora found Mrs Beam's directions easy to follow. It was a relief to get away from the gloomy cellar and her spirits were immediately lifted at the thought of doing something for herself. Independent at last, she thought, as she made her way through the bustling streets. I'm beholden to no one and back in the city where I was born. It was beginning to feel like an adventure, the start of a new story.

She found Mite Street and spotted the pawnbroker's shop at the sign of three golden balls, next door to a gin shop. Although it was only mid-morning, half a dozen men and women sat on the pavement, drinking outside.

Cora was a few paces away when she noticed a young, shabbily-dressed couple pause at the pawnbroker's door. The man turned to the woman with a beseeching expression but she twisted away and Cora noticed her eyes were red from crying. She wondered what their story was, what unfortunate circumstances had brought them here. Not wanting to push past them in their distress, Cora stepped into an alley running along the side of the shop and pretended to examine an advertising poster on the wall. She watched from the corner of her eye as the man took the woman's arm and pulled her close.

'We agreed now, Emily,' he said urgently. 'You promised.' The woman buried her head in her hands and began to cry. He looked about in agitation and drew her away from the noisy drinkers, unaware of Cora's presence nearby.

'Isn't there any other way?' she pleaded.

'It's only a ring!' The man rubbed his forehead despairingly. 'I'll find work, I promise. Then we'll get it back. If we don't pay the rent tomorrow we'll be out on the street. It's your choice, Emily.' The woman started to sob again.

'I'll not give my name,' she said, sniffing as she took a hankie from her purse to dry her eyes. 'I couldn't bear the shame of it.'

'People like us can't afford shame,' said the man miserably.

'Well, they'll not have my name. You must let me keep that, Freddie, at least.' With a deep breath she took his arm and straightened her jacket.

Cora admired her silent dignity. As they entered the pawnbroker's shop, she emerged from the alley and slipped in behind them.

The shop was cluttered and musty-smelling and appeared to be crammed with every human possession imaginable. Cora gazed in fascination; coal scuttles, cradles, fire tongs and fiddles, mousetraps, washboards and wooden legs were piled on shelves and stacked against the walls; the window was heaped with gaudy jewellery and the ceiling couldn't be seen for all the birdcages, carpet beaters and saucepans that hung from its beams. She ran her fingers across a dusty lampshade. It was as if someone had shaken a house until everything had fallen out of the cupboards.

Towards the far end of the shop a long counter divided the public space and an open office beyond, where the walls were covered with shelves and cubby-holes, methodically packed with bundles of all shapes and sizes.

There was no one inside so the young couple stepped up to the counter to wait, staring straight ahead to avoid Cora's eye as she took her place beside them.

A door opened at the back of the office and a short, pinch-faced man in a black shabby tailcoat entered the office, carrying a book as big as a family Bible. He walked straight past Cora and the young couple without giving them a glance and set the book down on a long desk that ran the length of one wall. Perching on a stool, he proceeded to thumb through the pages. When he found the place he was looking for, he opened an ink pot, brandished his quill with a flourish as if he was signing an important treaty, and began to write.

Cora noticed a bell on the counter but didn't feel bold enough to ring it. Something told her this man would ignore them for even longer if he was disturbed. Out of the corner of her eye she watched the tiny movement of the woman twisting the ring on her finger.

They waited and waited. The ticking of a dozen clocks bore into Cora's head. She began to lose her nerve. All she could think about was Elijah's delighted face the day he'd opened his parcel of handkerchiefs. Wasn't she betraying him now, bringing them to pawn for whatever she could get? But he wouldn't want you to starve, she told herself firmly, and he's not here now. *Elijah's left you nothing but memories.* At that moment the man ostentatiously put down his pen and came over to the counter. He stared down his nose at the young couple.

'New customers?'

Cora guessed this must be Snub, the man Mrs Beam had warned her about. He certainly enjoyed making people feel unimportant. She disliked him at once.

Just then, the door at the back of the office opened and a boy who looked about Cora's age ambled in, carrying a tiny monkey in his arms.

Cora had never seen a real monkey before, only a picture in one of Elijah's scientific books. It clung to the boy's waistcoat like a child, dressed in a scarlet jacket with two brass buttons and a scrap of gold braid on one cuff. She was captivated by the monkey's bright, intelligent face and delicate movements. The boy carried it to an old armchair beside an oil stove in the corner of the office. As soon as he sat down the monkey darted its tiny hand into his pocket and tugged out a paper bag. Peanuts spilled out and scattered across the floorboards. Snub swung round and directed a terse, irritated cough at the pair, but neither paid him any attention. The monkey jumped down to eat the peanuts off the floor and the boy took an apple out of another pocket and sat back to eat that himself, with a rebellious gleam in his eye.

Snub turned back to the man and his wife. 'What have you brought?' he said sharply.

49

'My wife has something to pledge,' the man replied, trying to master the desperation in his voice. His wife calmly slid the ring off her finger and gave it to Snub, who held it up to the light with a squint.

The boy looked up and saw Cora watching him. He wiped the juice from his mouth with the back of his hand and smiled. She realised she'd been staring and felt her cheeks flush.

'I shall need my eyeglass.' Snub put the ring down on the counter to search his pockets. In an instant the monkey leapt across the room, sprang onto the counter and grabbed the ring in his tiny fist.

The woman screamed and chaos broke out. Snub tried to grab the monkey but fell over his high stool. The husband reached out for its tail and missed.

'Pip!' cried the boy. 'Give it back!' But Pip just squeaked with delight and waved his prize in the air.

Cora couldn't help laughing. Pip was having too much fun to give his new treasure back. He bounded off the counter and landed right at her feet.

'Grab the ring,' shouted Snub, but before she could reach down Pip was already gone, leaping up into the window display, where he put a gold watch chain around his neck and sat applauding himself, to the delight of two children peering in from the street.

'Get it back!' cried the woman.

'Give it back, you little thief,' roared her husband, but Pip was too quick. He darted away once more and scrambled up to a high shelf where he climbed into a chamber pot and crouched, peeping over the rim with glinting eyes.

Cora felt sorry for the woman, who was no longer able to stop herself from crying. All this shouting isn't helping, she thought, it's frightening the monkey. She climbed onto a trunk and spoke softly. 'Come on, Pip.' She slowly stretched up her hand. 'There's a good boy. Show me what you've got in your pocket.' The monkey raised his head and tipped it to one side, quizzically. He was distracted by the boy opening a flap in the counter.

'Just grab the pot,' shouted the man impatiently. 'Can't somebody control that creature?'

Suddenly the boy was at Cora's side. 'Offer him these,' he said, holding up a fistful of raisins. 'Go on. Just talk to him nice.' He gave her an encouraging nod. Gripping the shelf with one hand to steady herself, Cora reached down and opened her palm for the raisins, then offered them up to the monkey.

'Look, Pip,' she said. 'Lovely raisins. Give me the lady's ring.'

Pip made an excited squeaking sound. He reached out of the chamber pot but Cora quickly moved her hand away. 'Give me the ring first.' Pip looked hurt.

'Doesn't he understand?' she asked the boy.

'Oh, he knows what you want all right!'

Sure enough, Pip gave a comical shrug and climbed out. Balancing on the edge of the shelf, he took the ring out of his pocket and dropped it into Cora's hand then set about picking out the raisins and stuffing them all into his mouth at once.

She felt his tiny fingers tickle her hand with delight.

When all the raisins were gone, Cora handed the ring to the woman. To her astonishment, Pip climbed lightly onto her shoulders and dropped into her arms. Beaming with pleasure, Cora nestled the little monkey and stroked its silky head. It seemed so delicate she was afraid she'd crush it.

'Oh, thank you!' The woman sighed with relief.

'He likes you,' said the boy, taking Cora's arm awkwardly to help her down from the trunk. Cora felt herself blush again. It felt good to be free at last in the weird, wonderful world. The monkey put its arms around her neck and nibbled her ear.

'I like you too, Pip,' she said. 'Even if you are a thief!'

Meanwhile the ring was returned to Mr Snub. He gave the boy a stern look. 'Unless you teach that ape how to behave, I'll give him to the butcher!'

'Do you hear that, Pip?' the boy whispered. 'You'll have to sleep on a bed of onions in a monkey pie!' A mock frown crumpled his brow, followed by a mischievous grin.

Cora wondered about the boy's relationship to the sour-faced shopkeeper. Mr Snub seemed to be in charge, but the boy didn't behave like his assistant. She liked his conspiratorial friendship with Pip. How lucky to have such a lively, affectionate companion.

Mr Snub straightened his neckerchief with great annoyance and turned his attention back to his customers.

Cora sat down on the trunk to play with Pip in her lap and wait her turn. 'What's your name?' she asked the boy.

'Joe,' he replied. 'Thanks for being kind to my friend here. He is a little thief but he don't know any different.'

'You mustn't steal, Pip,' scolded Cora, tapping him gently on the nose. 'It says so in the Bible. Don't you monkeys read the Bible?'

Joe laughed. 'He used to work for Mr Antonio, the organ grinder, collecting money from the crowd. Pa says he really just distracted everyone so that Mr Antonio's boy could pick their pockets. He loves anything shiny.'

'But why do you have him in here?'

'Mr Antonio brought him in with the organ, but he never came back.'

Poor Pip, thought Cora, gazing into his dark, round eyes. You were abandoned, just like me.

Just then the door opened and a small man in a neat suit came in.

'Watch,' whispered Joe.

When the young couple left, the man produced a ticket and repaid his loan. Mr Snub entered it in his book, then reached for a long cane, which he rapped on the edge of the shelves. At once Pip went to him. Mr Snub touched a parcel high on the top shelf with the end of the cane and Pip climbed up, fetched it down as if it were a coconut from a tree and put it on the counter.

'There, you see,' said Joe. 'He's very useful around here. It saves my father having to go up the ladder.'

'Is that him?' Cora wondered how such an easy-natured boy could have such a mean-spirited father.

'Crikey! No, that's Snub.' Joe frowned. 'I don't care if he falls off the ladder!'

He's very daring, speaking so loud, thought Cora, but she admired Joe's boldness.

'Snub's aunt owns this place and one day it'll belong to him,' explained Joe, beckoning to Pip. 'My father just works here. Snub has other lodgings, so we live upstairs, over the shop.'

The monkey scampered back to them. He caught sight of Cora's bag and reached for the shiny clasp.

Cora lifted it out of his reach. 'There's nothing in there for you, Pip!'

'Have you brought something to pawn?' asked Joe.

'The lady who told me to come here said I should talk to Mr Tally – is he your father?'

'Yes,' said Joe, 'he'll be back soon. So, who do you work for?'

She hesitated. *He thinks I've been sent on an errand for somebody else.* What should she say? Certainly not that she'd been abandoned and was sleeping in a cellar with tramps. She wanted him to like her. No one had ever been so friendly, so easy to talk to.

'I live with a teacher,' she said, thinking of Elijah. 'I'm a companion. I help teach the children to read.' It was a harmless story. Not so much a lie as an old truth.

'What's your name?'

The words came to her lips as if they had been waiting to hear themselves spoken. 'My name is Carrie.'

7

'Pip can do tricks,' said Joe proudly. 'Do you want to see some while you wait for my pa?'

Cora nodded happily.

'Sit there, then.' Joe picked up a violin case from the shelf and took out a bow.

'Watch this …' He knelt, holding the bow out at arm's length and clicked his tongue. Pip bounded into the air, somersaulted over the bow and bounced across the floor as if he were made of rubber. The monkey spun around and clapped, pleased with himself.

Cora laughed, and realised she'd forgotten how good it felt.

Joe raised the bow, an inch higher, then another, and each time Pip flung himself over, and never missed once.

As they talked, all thoughts of the miserable cellar of Farthing Court disappeared from Cora's mind. She was Carrie now, the schoolteacher's companion, sent on an errand without a worry in the world.

Half an hour later a middle-aged man in a threadbare overcoat and knitted scarf entered the shop, humming gently to himself.

'Here's Pa now,' said Joe.

Cora got to her feet and dusted down her skirt, feeling awkward that she'd been caught rolling marbles across the floor for Pip. But Mr Tally took in the game at once and smiled approvingly. He had the same kind eyes as Joe.

Mr Tally relieved Snub of his duties and hung up his coat in the office where he exchanged his felt hat for a velvet smoking cap with a gold tassel.

'Did you find old Mrs Melrose, Pa?' asked Joe, gathering up the marbles.

'Yes, I found her house on Buttle Street eventually,' replied his father, taking a stubby pencil and a ball of string out of a drawer. 'The poor woman had quite forgotten where she'd left her parcel. That's our good deed for the day.'

Mrs Beam was right, thought Cora. The two pawnbrokers were as different as chalk and cheese.

Joe gestured to Cora to show his father what she'd brought. Shyly she put her bag on the counter and took out the handkerchiefs. Despite her resolve, the sight of them filled her with sadness. There were the tiniest, most difficult stitches, the now imperceptible spot where she'd pricked her finger and had to wash away a stain. How could she hand them over? They're only scraps of linen, insisted a voice inside her head.

'This is Carrie, Pa,' said Joe. 'She's a friend of Pip's.' That was it. She was Carrie here. Cora suddenly felt stronger. These belong to your mistress, she told herself. Pass them across the counter, that's what you came to do.

'Well, here's some pretty work,' said Mr Tally, putting on his spectacles. He gave the handkerchiefs much consideration. Soon Cora had a ticket and fourpence in her pocket.

'Tell your mistress that we'll always pay for good linen,' he said. Cora thanked him. The weight of the pennies in her pocket cheered her up.

Joe walked with her to the door to say goodbye. 'Come back soon,' he said, '… to see Pip, I mean. You can teach him to read the Bible and learn not to steal!'

Cora walked down Mite Street with a spring in her step. I've got fourpence in my pocket and two new friends, she thought, as she skipped out of the path of a milk cart and crossed over to the sunny side of the street. It was a good start to the day. Next, she needed to find work, so she could pay for decent lodgings. Her short time at the pawnbroker's shop had set the scene for a new story. She imagined going to visit the shop on her days off work, playing with Pip and becoming friends with Joe.

Maybe he'd help her to find her way around the city. She felt far more at ease with him than Fletch. But why had she told Joe her name was Carrie? It was bad enough when other people used it. The name had come to her without thinking, as if it had spoken itself. Well, I'll just have to be Carrie when I'm there, she thought. What harm could come of it? The prospect of returning to Farthing Court after the warm, homely atmosphere of Mr Tally's shop soon dampened Cora's spirits. But now she had some money, at least she could pay her debt to Fletch. She came to a pie shop with an enticing display in the window and decided to buy a couple of mutton pasties.

When Cora entered the cellar she found Fletch, sitting deep in thought, idly tying knots in a piece of string.

'Where did you fly off to, Bird?' Fletch asked, eyeing Cora suspiciously. She pulled the string tight with a snap. 'You weren't thinking of leaving our little company? There ain't a safer place around for a girl like you.'

Cora sensed Fletch's three rules weren't the only conditions to her sanctuary in the cellar. Maybe she shouldn't have come back.

She offered Fletch the pies. 'Look, here's something in return for feeding me yesterday.' Fletch took them, but stowed them away without a nod of thanks.

'You got money, then?'

'No. I mean, yes.'

'Come in to some inheritance I s'pose, since I spent my last penny on your supper?'

Cora saw Fletch wouldn't be satisfied without an answer.

'Mrs Beam told me where to pawn some handkerchiefs. They gave me fourpence on them.'

'What else have you got in that bag, then?' Fletch reached for the bag, but Cora pulled it away. She wouldn't have anybody rifling through her things. They weren't much – the rag doll, a box, her little sewing case and a few clothes – but they belonged to her and Fletch had no right to ask for them.

'Just clothes,' she said. The bag made a thud as she put it down beside her.

'Clothes, eh. Clogs perhaps?'

There was a dangerous, challenging look in Fletch's eye. Cora didn't want to cross her. Reluctantly, she pulled out a wooden box with a faded painting of a windmill on the lid and held it close to her chest, making it clear that she wouldn't give it up. Nobody was going to touch the box that had belonged to her mother. It was her only keepsake.

'What's in it?'

Cora said the first thing that came into her head. 'Just hairpins and combs.' In truth she'd never been able to open the box and had no idea what it contained. Elijah had tried every key in the house, without any luck. One day she was determined to discover what her mother had kept inside, but for now she was happy just to hold it in her hands, knowing that her mother had held it too.

'Show me, then,' said Fletch.

'I can't, I lost the key.' Cora tried to sound as if it was unimportant.

'I'll break it open. Give it me.'

'No.' Cora clutched it tight. 'I don't want it broken. It was a present.'

'What use is a stupid box you can't open?'

Cora shrugged. At that moment, the boy with the twitch came down the steps, his dog limping along behind. Fletch got up to speak to him.

They muttered together in low voices, and Cora hurriedly put the box away, promising herself it would never leave her side as long as she was at Farthing Court. 'Shall we eat the pies?' she suggested, when Fletch returned.

'There's a better way you can pay for your keep.' Fletch picked up the string and thrust it into her pocket. 'Come with me, I've got a job to do.' It wasn't a request, it was a demand.

'What are we going to do?' Cora asked brightly, trying to appear willing after their confrontation over the box.

'You'll see,' said Fletch in a more friendly manner. 'It won't take long. But you'll have to leave the bag.'

So, it's a test, thought Cora. She put the bag inside the tea chest and looked around for something to hide it. There seemed to be nothing better than her cloak, so she crumpled that up and lay it on top then, as an afterthought, picked some chicken bones and apple cores off the floor and tossed those in too, to make it look like a box of rubbish. Still feeling uneasy, she followed Fletch out of the room.

Fletch led the way across the court without a word. When they reached the entrance to the passage she stopped and checked her pockets. Out came the string, bits of bent wire, some coins, screws and a handful of dirty humbugs. Cora was surprised to see how many pockets she had.

'There's something I left behind,' said Fletch, stuffing

them all back with an annoyed frown. 'Wait here.'

Cora leaned against the wall, wondering what she would have to do to pay her debt and free herself from Fletch. Her mind drifted as she watched a coalman's donkey pull his cart into the yard.

'Watch yer back!' A voice rasped behind her.

She spun round. The old sailor Fletch had spoken to the day before stepped out of the shadows and felt blindly around for his barrel seat. Cora took his arm and guided him to it.

'You're Fletch's girl, ain't yer?'

She didn't like the way he made it sound as though Fletch owned her.

'No,' she said. 'I'm just staying a few days, 'til I can sort myself out.'

He settled himself and pulled a pipe and tobacco pouch out of his pocket. 'Country girl, eh?'

Cora didn't like the sound of that either. 'No,' she repeated firmly. 'I was born here.'

'You can't fool me, lass. I weren't always washed up in this stinking cove.' He reached out for her skirt and tugged her close. 'A word of warning …' Cora could smell the drink on his breath. She tried to pull away but he held her fast. 'You've coasted into dangerous waters, lass,' he whispered. 'Dangerous waters …' He let her go and began to fill his pipe.

'What do you mean?' Cora wasn't sure if there was any sense to his words, but she was intrigued.

Nelson didn't answer her. Instead, he suddenly dropped his pipe in his lap and began to sing. 'Oh, for a soft and gentle wind, I heard a fair one cry, but give to me the roaring breeze and the white waves heaving high.'

Then Cora felt Fletch's presence beside her.

'Let's be going,' she said quietly, leading Cora away by the elbow. 'Don't listen to him, all those years at sea addled his head.'

Despite their awkward exchange in the cellar, Cora couldn't help admiring the swagger in Fletch's walk as they set off, her confident air as if she owned the street. But she also remembered Mrs Beam's words. Fletch's kingdom was a dangerous world.

They walked for half an hour, leaving the slums and noisy crowds behind for quieter, more respectable streets, until they emerged in a genteel crescent beside a park.

'Where are we?' Cora gazed at the fine houses.

'It doesn't matter,' murmured Fletch. 'That house with the yellow door, see it?' Cora nodded. 'My uncle lives there. I've got to collect some papers of his and deliver them to his office.'

Cora was suspicious at once. Why would Fletch be living in the rookery if she had an uncle who owned a house like that? It didn't make sense.

'What do you want me to do?'

'Put your hand inside the letterbox and grab the key – it's hanging there on a piece of string.'

'Why didn't your uncle give you a key?' The truth started to dawn.

Fletch glared at her. 'Just do as you're told,' she growled. 'My hand's too big. Yours will be small enough. Pull up the key then leave the rest to me.'

Cora felt sick. They walked towards the house in silence. She swallowed hard, trying to control her panic. Out of the corner of her eye she saw Fletch flex her fingers, shaking out the tension, her face drawn, eyes alert. *She doesn't care whether I believe her or not.* They reached the steps. Fletch looked at her hard. 'You owe me a favour, right?' she hissed between clenched teeth. 'Do as I say and there won't be any trouble.'

Cora nodded, her stomach knotted tight. This was wrong, she couldn't do it. She hesitated, but Fletch was already grabbing her by the arm and pulling her up the steps.

Fletch glanced over her shoulder. The street was quiet. At one end a nurse was taking some children into the park, at the other a woman was buying pot plants from a barrow. Fletch shoved Cora hard against the door. 'Do it. Now.'

Cora pushed her hand through the letterbox, her fingers trembled as she groped for the string, which was exactly where Fletch had said it would be. As soon as she pulled the key out Fletch snatched it, unlocked the door and slipped inside the house. 'Keep watch,' she snapped.

Cora sat down on the top step with the door ajar at her back, her pulse racing. What had she done? The thud of Fletch running up stairs inside brought her to her senses. *Don't just sit here looking suspicious, do something.* She pretended to tie her bootlace, hoping anyone who saw her would think she was waiting for the owner to come outside. What would happen if they were caught? Prison? It was only her second day in the city and here she was, breaking into a house. *I don't want to do this. I don't want to be like her.*

Cora scanned the empty street. This might be her only chance to escape. Save yourself now. She jumped up, darted down the steps and headed for the nearest side street. Her footsteps pounded the pavement so loudly she expected to see a face in every window. Then she came to a halt, heart thumping.

Her bag.

It was in the cellar and she had no idea how to get back there. She couldn't leave it behind, she had to go back. Stomach churning, mouth dry, Cora turned and started to walk towards the house as fast as she could, trying not to run, trying to control the panic taking hold.

As she got close, a carriage appeared at the far end of the road. She bowed her head and walked faster. Fletch had asked her to keep watch. What if this was the owner of the house returning? Should she try to warn her?

Cora reached the house just as the carriage approached, but without changing pace it rolled on past. The man inside stared intently at his newspaper and didn't stir. She ran up the steps, colliding with Fletch who was hurrying out.

'Let's go. Don't run. Don't look back.' Her breath was short, her voice urgent. She pulled her cap forward to hide her face. Cora lowered her head, praying that no one would see them, relieved that Fletch had no idea she'd run off. A moment later and she'd have caught her returning to the house.

With every step Cora expected to hear a shout or a cry of alarm. The crescent seemed to stretch forever. When at last they rounded the corner Fletch broke into a trot.

'Head for that church,' she cried, pointing to the nearest steeple rising above the rooftops. When they reached it they ran through a side gate into the graveyard and Fletch made for a dark, overgrown corner. She threw herself onto the grass, sweat streaming down her grimy face, and laughed triumphantly. Cora fell, breathless beside her.

'That was easy as picking daisies!' Fletch tugged a bulky napkin out of her jacket pocket. A dozen silver teaspoons and a pair of sugar tongs tumbled onto the grass. 'And there's more.' Her eyes gleamed with pride as she reached inside her jacket and produced a silver picture frame from one pocket and a pair of fine kid gloves from another. Cora watched Fletch examine her treasure excitedly.

'This lot'll fetch a shilling for the sweep's boy.' She picked up the sugar tongs, huffed on them and polished them on her sleeve. 'It was him told me about the key; he saw it hanging from the inside. We've got an understanding, see.' She held up the tongs to admire her work. 'He notices windows left open and houses empty all day. I do the job and pay him his cut. It's simple.' Fletch talked fast, exhilarated.

'When I saw your little hands I knew we could do it.'

Cora realised with a flash of anger that Fletch had planned to use her all along. 'Is that why you saved me from the kidsman?' she blurted.

Fletch turned on Cora. 'I saved you 'cos I needed a girl,'

she snarled, 'and there you was – thrown out of a carriage in front of the workhouse.'

Cora was unnerved. What did she mean, 'needed a girl'?

Fletch smirked. 'I didn't notice your hands 'til after.' She started shoving the spoons back into her pockets. 'We can work together, you and me,' she said. 'You'll earn that fourpence to re-pay the pawnbroker and more. There'll be lean times, all right, but you'll never starve, I'll see to it.' She seized Cora by the sleeves. 'You're lucky I picked you up, girl. Wherever you come from, you're nothing here. You'd be wishing you were dead already if that kidsman had got hold of you. And if he hadn't snatched you, there'd be another, even worse. But I'll teach you stuff. Two can work tricks. People will trust a girl like you, in your country frock.'

She tucked the picture frame back inside her jacket and scrambled to her feet. 'Course, they'd teach you stuff at Walston too, like how to pick oakum 'til your hands bleed or how to sleep with the mad ones screaming all night. Maybe you'd prefer that?' She held her hand out to Cora and grinned. 'Be smart, Bird. You don't want to starve or go crazy. You've got to look out for yourself, like me.'

Cora stared at the untended tombstones around them, overgrown with nettles. With a heavy heart she got to her feet and followed Fletch silently out of the graveyard.

 **8**

ora was relieved to find her bag still in its hiding place when they got back to the cellar. While Fletch emptied her pockets and parcelled up the stolen things in newspaper, Cora turned her back, gently twisted the clasp so that it wouldn't make a sound and opened the bag. She reached inside and touched every object with her fingertips, one by one. Each became a talisman. Belle's tiny stuffed hand, the braid on her old sewing case. They made her feel calm, sure of what was right and wrong again. And her mother's box.

'Hungry now?'

Cora shut the bag. Fletch retrieved the pies she'd bought earlier. They sat, side by side on the mattress, to eat. Fletch said nothing more about wanting Cora to help her.

She thinks I've got no choice, thought Cora, brooding resentfully over what had happened. She was even more determined not to be told what to do by anyone.

Fletch finished eating, gathered the paper parcels and wrapped them up in a sack.

'I've got to get rid of this stuff,' she said, getting up to leave. 'You bide here. The sort I'm going to see don't like hangers-on.'

Cora nodded. Now would be her chance to escape.

At the door Fletch paused and turned, as though Cora's thoughts had reached her. 'You won't last a week out there on your own, girl, remember that.'

When Fletch was gone Cora breathed freely. She wiped her greasy hands on her skirt and reached for the bag. Sitting back against the wall, she took out the windmill box, shook it and listened to the familiar rattle and rustle inside. The sound comforted her, talked to her in words she didn't understand. It told her there was something more to know. *Who are you, Cora Parry? Where do you come from? What's your real story?* A rat scurried over and started to gnaw at the edge of the mattress. Cora kicked it away. She stared at the box, still and silent in her hands. She would have to make up her own story now. Childish comforts couldn't help her any more.

A sudden scream echoed across the court followed by angry shouting. Cora was shaken from her thoughts. *I've got to get out of here.* She gathered up her things, grabbed her cloak and hurried towards the door. As her hand touched the handle she heard a frail cough.

'Ain't you staying, Miss?' The young mother, Nellie, looked up with dark, hollow eyes.

Cora paused and shook her head. She looked with pity at the woman's frail body, almost skin and bone.

Nellie stretched out a trembling hand. 'Take us with you. Please, Miss.'

'I can't ...' Cora tried not to sound impatient to get away, 'you're not well.'

'I know,' Nellie sighed. 'But Fletch keeps saying I've got to earn my keep, begging for her with the littl'un.' She shifted the baby from one arm to the other. 'I don't want to do it, Miss, but I owe her. If I could walk away like you ...'

Cora didn't know what to say. *There's nothing I can do for her.* All she could do was smile as she wrapped her cloak around her shoulders and hurried out of the cellar and across the yard, determined never to set foot in Farthing Court again.

Cora walked briskly away from the rookery and pulled her hood over her head, hoping she wouldn't meet Fletch in the street. When she came to the shadowy tunnel of a railway arch she dived inside.

Thank goodness I'm out of that place, she thought, collapsing against the wall. The cellar's foul smell still clung to her clothes. She wished she had others to change into so that she could throw these away and rid herself of the memory. A cold wind swept through the tunnel. Cora shivered. The edge of autumn would soon turn sharp. Was it only yesterday morning that Martha's brother had left her outside the workhouse? At least I'm better off than I was then, she reminded herself. I've met Joe and Pip and I've still got tuppence. She opened her bag and felt inside. Belle was there, the windmill box and everything else – but the coins were gone. Fletch! In a flash she remembered Fletch returning to the cellar that morning. All the fuss searching through her pockets – it had just been a trick! Cora thumped her fist against the wall. She wouldn't go back and be a thief's apprentice. She wouldn't let Fletch control her like this. She'd find her own way. But how? Cora thought of Nellie being sent out on the street with her baby, but she had her pride. *I'll never beg, never.* All she needed was a place to sleep and clean herself up so she could search for work. And for that she'd need rent money. Cora looked down at her bag again. Was there anything else she could bear to part with? Not Belle, or the windmill box. The sewing case might come in useful. Maybe she could do without the nightdress and sleep in her shift. The dress. Cora remembered her dream of the bright, sun-filled room. A face came to her mind, the face of the girl she'd seen in the carriage outside the workhouse, a girl so like herself she could have been a twin. I bet you sleep in a room like that, without a care in the world, she thought. We're two sides of a coin. Fate is kind to one and cruel to the other – you've got the easy life and I've got the street.

Well, it was time to take control of her own future. Cora pinned up her hair and picked up her bag. With a deep breath she stuck her chin in the air and headed for Mite Street.

When Cora arrived at the pawnbroker's shop she found it crowded with a dozen people waiting their turn. There was no sign of Joe or Pip; Mr Snub was alone behind the counter. Cora took her place in the queue behind a woman with a pair of faded curtains over her arm. A pamphlet lying on one of the shelves caught her eye: 'The Dying Confession of Captain Rabb.' It was not the sort of tale that had ever entered Elijah's house. Curious, she picked it up and started to read.

Cora was soon so engrossed with Captain Rabb's confessions that she didn't notice the shop gradually empty, until only a couple of customers were left. Somebody brushed past her knee; Cora raised her eyes and saw a bent woman hobbling up to the counter. The woman cradled a bundle, hung across her body like a child in a sling, leaving one hand free to clutch her walking stick. With great difficulty she heaved the bundle onto the counter. As she did so her stick fell to the floor. Cora came to her aid.

'Bless you,' said the woman with a sigh.

Snub examined her bundle. 'I'll take the baking dish as usual,' he said, unfolding the clothes wrapped around it with a look of distaste. 'But you know you're wasting my time bringing these rags, Mrs Perkins. They're all worn to a thread. Put them back on your children. And the waistcoat – shabby. Not worth a penny.' He started to write a ticket for the dish.

'I'll take two shillings for the lot,' said the woman, grasping his arm desperately. But he shook her off without looking her in the eye.

'A shilling then, ninepence? How will I put bread on the table for my little ones, Mr Snub, Sir?'

Snub counted out fourpence for the dish from his money drawer, pushed it across the counter and looked directly over her shoulder.

'Next!' he snapped. Cora watched indignantly. A few pennies are nothing to him and everything to people like that. Like us, she thought, with a jolt. She could only look on as Mrs Perkins bundled up the rejected clothes and hung them once more around her neck. Although her burden was lighter, she left bowed even lower than before. The next customer took her place.

'I've come for my saw, Mr Snub, Sir.' He laid his ticket and some coins on the counter.

'You're a ha'penny short,' said Snub, glaring over the top of his glasses.

'It's all I got.' The man stared awkwardly at his boots. 'I've found a week's work, so I can settle up when I'm paid, Mr Snub. But I can't work without the saw, Sir.'

'And I can't give it to you without the ha'penny,' insisted Snub. 'You know the rules.'

'How can I pay if I can't work?' The man thumped his fists on the counter. 'I'll lose that job without my saw! You heartless devil ... you ...'

The man began to roll up his sleeves and threatened to climb over the counter, but just at that moment, the door at the back of the office opened and Joe and his father appeared. At once Snub saw his chance to extricate himself and scuttled to the back of the room to fuss about with some parcels. Joe noticed Cora and his face broke into a broad grin.

Cora smiled back and waited her turn, relieved she'd been spared Snub's humiliation.

Now that Mr Tally took over at the counter, the man calmed down and explained his problem.

'How much is the saw worth?'

'One shilling,' said Joe, reading the ticket.

'Well, as it happens I've a saw myself,' said Mr Tally. 'I don't use it much. We'll exchange for a week, shall we, Mr Barlow? I know a man likes to use his own tools. Fetch the saw, Joe.'

'You'll have it back by Sunday,' promised Mr Barlow. He shook Mr Tally's hand vigorously. 'You're a fine man, Mr Tally, Sir. A fine, generous man. God bless you.'

If only Joe's father had been there when Mrs Perkins

brought in her bundle, thought Cora. I'm sure he wouldn't have refused her other things.

Joe lifted the flap in the counter, unbolted the hatch below and came through into the shop to see Cora.

'You're back soon.'

'I forgot to bring something.' The lie caught in her throat, but it was too late to unpick what she'd said.

Joe noticed the pamphlet in her hand. 'What's that?' he asked.

'It's the confession of a ship's captain who was hanged for being a smuggler,' said Cora. 'He lived a double life until they caught him.'

Joe took the pamphlet and studied the crude portrait of the captain on the cover. 'Ain't you working today?'

'No.' At least that's true, Cora thought. 'It's a day off,' she added.

'Will you read this to me, then?' asked Joe.

She was caught by surprise, but pleased to be asked. 'Can't you read it yourself?'

'No one ever learned me.'

The doorbell rang. A man clutching an empty parrot cage came into the shop, followed by another, carrying a euphonium.

'Wouldn't we be in the way?' whispered Cora.

'There's a store room out the back,' said Joe. 'We wouldn't disturb anyone there. If it gets busy in the shop again Pa can just shout.'

It would be good to stay a while. The pawnbroker's shop was the only place where Cora had felt safe since she'd arrived in the city. With its tea-cosies and feather dusters, it seemed comforting after the subterranean gloom of Farthing Court.

'All right, I'll read it to you.'

Joe seemed pleased, and Cora followed him through a door at the back of the office into a dark, cramped hallway. A steep staircase rose ahead but Joe led her to the left, into a dusty store room lit by a barred, grimy window.

'I often sit in here when nobody needs me,' said Joe, showing her to a chaise longue sprouting its horsehair stuffing in the corner. Cora gazed at the neatly packed shelves that covered the walls from floor to ceiling, just like the office. Here there were also dividing walls, with narrow spaces between them. She wondered what some of the unusually shaped parcels might be.

Joe followed her eyes. 'It's like a museum, eh?' he said proudly. 'And this isn't all. There's two more rooms of it upstairs and the cellar's full below.'

They settled themselves on the chaise longue, which Joe had made comfortable with old bolsters. Cora opened the Captain's confession and began. Joe listened intently, leaning close now and then to peer at the cheap engravings of wrecks and smugglers, and Cora remembered how she used to shut her eyes when Elijah read to her, letting his voice conjure pictures in her imagination. It was such a long time since she'd shared a story.

Joe wouldn't let Cora stop until the grisly end. 'Do you think it's all true?' he asked, when she'd finished.

'He had a lot of lucky escapes,' said Cora. 'I'm not sure I believe all of them.'

'Will you read it again?' Joe turned the closed book over in her lap.

She laughed. 'No, not today, but it's a good one,' she agreed. 'I like sea stories.'

'I know a great sea story,' said Joe, 'a true one about my pa. He was a sailor in the navy when he was young. He won a medal for being a real hero.'

'What did he do?'

'He saved the captain's life when their ship went down off Biscay,' said Joe proudly. 'Pa pulled him onto the wreckage, even though his own leg was broke, and sailed it like a raft until a Spanish ship found them. All the rest of the crew drowned. They were the only survivors.'

'Somebody should write his story in a book,' said Cora. Joe beamed with pride.

'I'm going to learn reading and writing one day myself,' he said, 'but not to write stories. I've got plans, see. I don't want to work here for ever. At the moment my father's in charge, because he's been here a long time. Snub only came a year ago to learn the ropes. But one day he'll inherit this place and then our lives won't be worth living.'

Cora could easily imagine how unpleasant that might be.

'When I'm older I want to have a shop of my own,' explained Joe. 'A proper shop selling good second-hand stuff, real antiques, not old clothes and tin baths. If I could read documents and letters and the like, then I could have my own business. I'm going to make my pa proud. When he's old I'll be able to see him right, just like he's looked after me, just like he deserves.'

For a moment Cora felt a pang of jealousy. Joe had a father who was a real hero, somebody he admired. Not like her own father, whoever he was.

'I'm going to make something of myself, for Pa,' said Joe with a frown. 'That counter in the shop is only a yard wide but I don't want us to be on the other side of it one day.'

That's my place, thought Cora. Thank goodness he didn't know the truth.

Joe suddenly looked awkward. He picked at a loose end of wool hanging off his sleeve. 'Would you teach me reading?' he asked.

'Well …' Cora hesitated. She'd love to teach Joe, but how could she make him a promise? She didn't even know where she was going to sleep that night.

'I'll pay you,' said Joe. 'I've got money saved from working. How much do the others pay?'

For a moment she was puzzled, then she remembered what she'd told him about being a teacher's companion. That stupid lie.

'All right,' she said. 'I won't be able to come every day, but I can give you a lesson whenever I'm free.' It wasn't so far from the truth anyway. She had helped Elijah in the schoolroom sometimes.

'That's great!' Joe beamed. His excitement was infectious and it gave Cora an idea. Why not become a teacher? There were sure to be others who would pay for lessons. She could read and write well, and Elijah would be proud of that. Suddenly she saw a vision of the future, something to work towards, and for now, at least, it would give her a reason to spend more time with Joe and Pip at the shop.

'Just give me what you can afford,' she said, wishing she didn't need to take his money.

Joe nodded enthusiastically and dropped the pamphlet back in her lap. 'Can we start right now?'

An hour later, Joe had mastered half the alphabet with Cora's help from the pages of the captain's confessions and paid her a penny for it.

'You're looking pleased with yourself,' said Mr Tally, as Joe led Cora back into the shop, which was now empty. They heard a squeak and the tiny monkey, who'd been asleep in the cupboard under the stairs, scampered in after them.

'We've been teaching Pip tricks, Pa,' said Joe quickly.

Cora smiled secretly. She wasn't the only one to find a lie useful. The thought made her feel a little less guilty.

Mr Tally picked up Pip and swung him onto his shoulders. 'If only you'd teach him accounts we could all go on holiday,' he said, laughing. 'Did you come back just to see Pip or have you brought something else to pledge, my dear?'

Cora pulled the nightdress out of her bag. 'You were very kind to help that man with his saw,' she said, before he could ask any awkward questions.

'Well, all Snub understands is profit,' said Mr Tally handing Pip to Joe. 'This place will be his one day so he wants it ticking over nicely. He doesn't want to be known for charity.' Mr Tally looked at the dress and reached out for a ticket. 'But that's not how things are for the people round here. It's more of a service, you see, and many of them rely on it.' He took out a handkerchief and cleaned his spectacles. 'Mrs Percy's baking dish, for example; she will always bring it in on a Thursday morning because her husband's wages never last any longer. But as soon as he's been paid at the end of the week she'll be back for it, just in time to fill it with scraps from the butcher for their Sunday lunch. Same with all these Sunday suits. Men rely on the money they can borrow on them. They only need their suits one day a week. We make our pennies and they can feed their children.'

'What about the saw?' asked Cora, fascinated to hear the role the kindly pawnbroker played in people's lives.

'You can tell the state of business in this city by the tools that come in,' said Mr Tally, shaking his head sadly. 'First a man brings in a tool he hardly uses. Then another and another. Finally, when there's no work around for him to do, or he's too sick to do it, he brings his most valuable tool. Maybe it's been passed down from father to son, like that saw. You don't expect to get your money back on that. But if a man finds work, like our friend there, then it's a Christian duty to help him. Help him raise himself up. That's what Snub doesn't care about. He only cares to raise himself. Every drab little shawl, every chisel and worn pair of shoes on these shelves tells a human story. All the woes and worries of mankind are here, Miss Carrie. And all its treasures too.'

He handed her four coins and a ticket. Cora thanked him. As she slipped the coins into her pocket she took one last look at her nightdress, soon to join the sad company of unclaimed items for sale.

'You'll come back soon,' said Joe at the door. 'Whenever your mistress don't need you?'

Cora saw the dream alive now in his eyes. 'Yes, I'll come, whenever I can.'

Cora said goodbye for the second time that day and stepped out into the street. Hope glimmered in her heart. All the possibilities of the city lay ahead of her. Cora took a deep breath and held her head high. Which way, left or right? She didn't care. All that mattered was to begin.

9

ora bought herself a pennyworth of whelks from a shellfish barrow and strolled along the street as she ate. Ahead, she heard the murmur of lively voices and music and soon found herself in a large open square, where a company of street entertainers was performing.

Cora sauntered happily among the sea of faces. It felt good to be part of the crowd. Here she was, stepping into her new story. Carrie's story. She felt strong, independent. She'd make a respectable life for herself in this city.

A pair of stilt walkers dressed in harlequin coats towered over them all, rocking on their stiff legs. Cora remembered seeing a stilt walker in the village once, when he came to advertise a travelling fair. It was one of her greatest triumphs that Martha had never discovered she'd sneaked out that night to watch the forbidden show through a hole in the tent. Now here she was, moving among the performers as she pleased, excited by the smells, the sights and sounds of the fair. Bagpipes and hurdy-gurdys rang out above the noise. On she went, from one wonder to another: a sword swallower lowered a long blade deep into his throat right before her eyes; a trio of dogs walked on their hind legs, balancing balls on their noses; buskers and ballad singers competed for an audience and jugglers tossed skittles high above the crowd. All the while a succession of spectators gasped and roared, moving happily along from one feat to the next.

Cora wandered through the fair until she heard a voice she recognised, booming above the hubbub.

'Marvel at the magic, be amazed by the mystery! Prepare to be baffled, bamboozled and bemused!'

That's Mordecai Beam, she thought with a smile. Cora pulled up the hood of her cloak to conceal herself and searched him out. At first she couldn't see him for the crowd that had gathered round, but pushing close to the front she caught sight of him sitting under an arcade at the edge of the square, with a gaily painted tray on his knees. She scanned the scene for a stooped, brooding figure loitering in a doorway, but Fletch was nowhere to be seen. Don't be stupid, Cora told herself. There's no reason why she should be hanging around here. Still, she shuddered at the thought of meeting Fletch again.

Mordecai began a trick with three cups and a ball. Cora shrank back behind a pillar and watched him put the ball beneath one of the cups and then slide all three around the tray, talking all the while about Lady Luck and 'the hand being faster than the eye'.

'And now, for a volunteer.' A man stepped forward to choose which cup concealed the red ball. He made a show of boasting to the crowd that he couldn't be fooled. But Mordecai played him like a fish on a line, tipping the cups, letting him believe, stalling, whipping up the crowd for and against his victim's choice, until at last he revealed – the hand was indeed faster than the eye! To the man's astonishment, the ball was safely hidden in another cup. Cora clapped and whistled with the rest. Mrs Beam was right, she thought, people were giving Mordecai their money and he deserved it for his showmanship. As the boys appeared with a collecting tin she slipped out of sight.

The clatter of coins in the tin brought Cora up sharp. *I shouldn't be standing here watching Mordecai make money, I've got to find a way to earn some myself.* Church bells chimed five o'clock. She needed to find lodgings if she wanted to have somewhere to sleep that night. It wouldn't be possible to get work as a teacher straight away. The only skills Martha had taught her were cooking and cleaning – surely they would be useful somewhere?

Cora was afraid of straying too far from Mite Street for fear of being unable to find Joe and the pawn shop again, but the streets around the square seemed to be filled with tea merchants, bookstalls and tobacconists, without any sign of the sort of place where she might find work. She ventured on and found herself among theatre buildings and music halls. In the side streets there were plenty of grubby cards in cracked windows advertising lodgings, but they were low-looking establishments. Gaudy women slouched in the doorways, glaring sullenly as she passed while men sat out, smoking and drinking. Cora was unnerved by the brooding, predatory atmosphere there and walked quickly on.

Feeling hungry and tired, she came to a large, busy chop house and decided to give it a try. At least she might get fed here if she got a job. Gathering up her courage she went in and approached the man who looked as though he was in charge.

'Experience?' he said, rapping a menu on the counter impatiently.

'Oh, nothing ...' Cora hadn't expected this question. 'But I can wash up.' She smiled hopefully.

'No good to me. Try next door.' He turned on his heel and disappeared into the kitchen.

She tried next door at Billing's Fish Dinners, but they had all the staff they needed. A few doors down she asked in Polly's Tea Shop but they had a waiting list for jobs.

The early autumn evening drew in. Lamps were lit, candles glowed. Cora realised her hope of finding work was fading. Maybe the money she'd got left from Mr Tally would be enough for something cheap to eat and a bed for the night. She retraced her steps to the square where there had been food of every kind for sale. A man selling sausages had put a couple of split ones aside. She stood at the edge of his barrow and waited to catch his eye.

'Please, Sir, can I buy those?' Cora pointed, hoping that she looked as hungry as she felt. The man continued serving, but called out to his boy.

'Give her the splits, Jakey, half price.' A thin, spotty

youth, who'd been talking to a friend, gave a resentful shrug, came over and wrapped up the sausages.

'That's tuppence then.' He held out his hand for the money with a superior smirk. He knows I can't afford the good ones, thought Cora, annoyed, as she reached into her pocket. But the pocket was empty.

'Hurry up, I ain't got all day,' he scowled as she tried the other pocket in vain.

'I haven't …' Cora stuttered, 'I can't …'

'Don't try and pull that one on me, we ain't charity.' He cast the parcel aside.

'I don't want charity …' Cora felt her eyes well up. She turned away in frustration and pushed her way out of his sight, into the crowd. How could I have been so stupid, losing my money twice in one day? It must have been a pickpocket when she'd stopped to watch the cup trick. Now she'd have no supper and no bed that night. Who could she ask for help? If she went back to Mite Street and told Joe the truth, maybe Mr Tally would help her. But what would he think when he found out that she'd lied? She didn't want to lose the only friend she had.

Cora walked aimlessly among the crowd, feeling desperate and alone. As the night grew darker, the city let slip its reveller's mask and revealed a more brutal face. The juggling boys and stilt walkers were gone. In their place were liquor stalls, freak shows and grotesque spectacles, mobbed by a mass of people who had been drinking all afternoon and were now a loud, raucous rabble.

Cora was pushed and shoved from every side by coarse women shrieking with laughter and staggering, red-faced men bellowing like bulls, all of them lurching and leering, wild-eyed. Everything spun around her, larger than life, cruel and raw. She headed for a side street, but a gang of men betting on a dogfight blocked the way. She tried another, but a riot of people were arguing over a squealing pig.

The high-spirited crowd she'd joined that afternoon had turned into a carnival of beasts in the night. Cora started to run, pushing past people, taking any turn. *Run, run.* If only she could run out of her impossible life and escape into another.

≈ 10 ≈

Cora awoke at first light, shivering in the cold. Her legs ached with cramp. She had spent the night under a church portico, tucked in the shelter of a wall, but it had not turned out to be a peaceful refuge. In the early hours, a pair of drunks had staggered up the steps and collapsed in a heap close by, where they lay, mumbling fragments of a miserable song. With her bag hidden under her cloak Cora had kept as still as a mouse, wedged against the hard stone until she was numb and chilled to the bone.

Now the two drunkards lay sprawled in an unconscious heap and she saw that several other people had joined them while she'd been asleep. To her surprise she noticed Marnie among them, sitting against a pillar, snoring peacefully, surrounded by her bags and baskets. Cora wondered what this child-like woman did all day and why she slept out when she had a place in the cellar. But she wasn't going to wait here to find out. Stepping carefully, Cora managed to make her way down the steps without disturbing anyone. She felt dirty and humiliated. First a thieves' den, now a night among tramps. She had to find work and a bed for tonight, no matter what.

The aroma from a coffee house tempted her close. Would they need someone to wash up? She stared through the window at people eating their breakfast rolls. Cora took a deep breath and went inside. She hadn't noticed how filthy she was from her night on the street. Her clothes were smeared with fairground food and the church portico, strewn with damp, rotting leaves, had made it worse. Somewhere she had lost her cap and her lank, unwashed hair hung loose. The proprietor of the coffee house looked at her with disapproval and turned her away.

He treated me like a nobody, she thought, as she walked away, rubbing angry tears from her eyes. It was the same at the next coffee house and everywhere she went. Although she brushed the dirt off her cloak and tied up her hair as best she could, Cora was told she wasn't fit to work in any kitchen, not presentable enough to work in a shop and too scrawny to be of use to anyone at the market.

The morning wore on without success and Cora became more and more dispirited. By chance, she found herself taking a turn into Mite Street and walking up the road towards the pawnbroker's shop once again. Staying out of sight behind a bookstall, she stared through the window.

Joe was busy sweeping the floor while Pip played with a ball of screwed-up paper. She felt a pang of loneliness and desperately wanted to go in, to sit among the pots and pans and listen to Joe's easy talk, to hold Pip and feel his little arms around her neck, to be Joe's friend Carrie, the teacher's companion without a care in the world.

She caught sight of her reflection in the window of the gin shop next door. It was true, she did look like a tramp. Joe's words echoed in her head, 'I don't want to be on the other side of that counter one day'. She couldn't bear to go in and tell him the truth. She wanted him to believe in Carrie. It made her feel she was somebody worthwhile – not some street girl. Cora rubbed the dirt from her face, brushed down her dress, and walked on.

At last Cora spotted a guesthouse with a sign in the window that said, 'Professions Only'. This time she crossed her fingers for luck behind her back and knocked on the door. The woman who opened it seemed surprised.

'Please, Ma'am, I'm looking for work,' said Cora earnestly. 'Live in. I'll do anything. Please, I'll work hard.' She managed a smile and stood with her shoulders back, desperately trying to look honest and strong.

'I'm afraid we don't need anyone here,' the woman replied with an apologetic smile. 'You know you should never knock at the front door, dear. Always go to the tradesman's for work.'

'Yes, Ma'am.' Cora's spirits sank. She blinked back tears. But the woman didn't immediately close the door. She hesitated, thoughtfully.

'Have you no family?' Cora shook her head. 'Wait here

a moment.' The woman disappeared up the stairs. Cora waited, wondering what was going to happen next. She peered inside the house. On the hall table was a vase of roses and a small silver tray. A voice whispered inside her head. *Fletch would take that and run. You could do it. Here's your chance to eat a hot meal and sleep in a bed tonight.* Cora's pulse started to race. Even if it wasn't real silver, it'd be worth something. *It's probably nothing precious to her but if I sold it I could eat for a week.* She stepped inside and listened. Silence. She moved towards the table and reached out. Her fingers touched the cold tray, but she couldn't take it. Something stronger than hunger held her back. If she stole it she'd be exactly the person Fletch wanted her to be. Cora darted back outside. She imagined Fletch laughing scornfully.

A few moments later the woman returned with a red woollen dress neatly folded in her arms. 'Take this,' she said. 'My daughter has just grown out of it.' Cora accepted the dress gratefully but couldn't look the woman in the eye.

'Thank you, thank you, Ma'am.' She stroked its fine cloth, the colour of field poppies, its scalloped collar and cuffs; her fingers trembled with shame at what she had almost done.

'I'm afraid you'll be lucky to find anyone who'll take you in off the street,' said the woman. 'You'd do best to go to Walston Workhouse. At least you'll get a meal and work there.'

Walston Workhouse.

Cora felt the words darken her mind like a shadow.

That place haunted her, whispering its name with so many voices. But she'd never walk through those gates. No matter what she had to do to survive. She'd never go back. Never.

Cora carefully laid the dress in her bag and thanked the woman again. 'Which way?' she said, wanting at least to appear grateful for the advice.

'Ask the newspaper boy on the corner,' the woman replied. 'He'll tell you.'

But Cora didn't ask. She didn't need to. She knocked on several more doors that morning, each in vain. Two hours later she turned a corner and found herself standing before the formidable arch of Walston Workhouse once more.

❧ 11 ❧

'God save their souls from the Devil's work!'
Cora looked up, startled. She hadn't
noticed an old woman stop beside her as
she leaned against the workhouse railings. The woman
paid no attention to Cora, but watched a covered wagon
being pulled across the yard by a starved-looking donkey.
A thin man with a stick tramped gloomily along beside it.

'They bring bones but they take away bodies.'

The words reminded Cora of something Martha had
once said. 'Why do they bring bones?' she asked.

'The poor beggars smash them up all day long, for
fertilizer,' the old woman replied. 'But what's coming out
in that wagon won't go on top of the soil – they'll bury
those bones six feet under.'

Cora shuddered. As the wagon rattled past them through the gate she almost expected to see a hand or a foot slip out from beneath the tarpaulin. Had her mother been taken away in the very same cart? She felt a desperate aching sadness. Where were they going to be buried, with no mourners, no dignity? If her mother hadn't taken that step across the threshold, maybe something, somebody might have saved her. She ignored the pangs of hunger gnawing at her stomach and turned her back on Walston. 'I know a woman who died there,' Cora said. 'She was already sick when she arrived.'

'Then it was a blessing.' The old woman took a small medicine bottle from a bag tied to her belt, pulled out the cork and took a swig from it. She wiped her lips with her apron. 'There's worse than death in that place.'

'What do you mean?' Cora was filled with dread.

'Goings on,' said the old woman darkly. 'Young women disappear – nobody knows what happens to them. They vanish in the night; four have gone since St Clare's Day, a month past.' She took another drink from the bottle and put it back in her bag. 'There's much worse than death for some.'

'Where do they go?'

The woman's eyes grew wide as if she was suddenly possessed. 'The Devil takes them,' she rasped, raising her hands before her face. 'I've seen it – the Devil's coach, with red serpents riding the wheels!'

Cora listened with a mixture of astonishment and fear. The Devil's coach. At once the story had a grip on her. 'Doesn't anyone see what happens?' she asked. The old woman pulled a tiny cross from around her neck, kissed it and tucked it away inside her bodice, muttering to herself. Without another word to Cora, she hobbled away.

What was the sinister secret of Walston Workhouse? Cora was sure something more powerful than chance kept drawing her back. She felt its cruelty, its menace. How hungry would she have to be, how dejected and afraid, before she was too weak to turn away? She sat on the pavement and hung her head in her hands. It was a bleak place to feel close to her mother but somehow, in her desperation, without anywhere else to go or anyone to turn to, she felt some pitiful comfort there. She didn't see the shadowy figure loitering in a dark passage on the opposite side of the road.

Fletch watched Cora all afternoon. She watched her while a hundred people walked past and nobody stopped to toss a coin in her lap. She watched her while a mad woman tried to steal Cora's bag and tussled for it, kicking her and spitting in her face. She watched Cora until hunger made her grey and hollow-eyed and the damp evening air made her shiver with cold. Then, as dusk fell, she crossed the street with a sweet apple dumpling.

∾ 12 ∾

Cora's return to Farthing Court was greeted with silent stares from the inhabitants of the cellar, but she was too dejected to notice. She was ashamed that she'd failed to look after herself, humiliated that she'd had to accept help from Fletch again.

Marnie shifted her baggage to make space for Cora and sprinkled a handful of dried leaves over her hair like a child playing with petals.

'Fletch has caught her little bird,' she said, fluttering her plump fingers. 'Poor little sparrow.'

Cora let the leaves fall around her. You're right, Marnie, she thought miserably. I'm trapped like a bird in a cage. Now Fletch had caught her, she'd be punished, Cora was sure of that. Dust to dust, ashes to ashes, that's what the parson had said at Martha's funeral, we all return to our beginning. *Well, now I know what it's like to return to my beginning. I'm nobody, not worth a chance or charity. I might as well rot in this hole as in Walston.*

Fletch fetched Cora a dish of hot steak and kidney from the tavern and watched her eat it without a word. Cora knew she would have to pay for every mouthful but she ate hungrily.

When she'd finished eating Cora was overcome with exhaustion. Soft, melancholy notes of a harmonica drifted into the candlelit cellar. She lay down and pulled her cloak around her. After a cold, uncomfortable night outside the church, that thin mattress was as good as a feather bed. Fletch picked up her greatcoat and laid it over Cora's curled figure as carefully as she wrapped up her silver spoons.

'Sleep, Bird,' she said. 'Fletch'll look after you now.'

When Cora woke next morning, Fletch was gone. She sat up and rubbed the sleep from her eyes, shivering. The room was suffused with a soft, ochre light glowing through the brown paper at the window. Where the paper was torn she glimpsed slivers of crazed glass and a distortion of the cellar steps beyond.

Around her, the other inhabitants of the cellar were also waking, stretching and yawning, hiding their bedclothes under crates and boxes or bundling up their tatty blankets.

She could just walk out, up those steps and away. Nobody would stop her. And yet Cora couldn't move. All her resolve, all her hope of the day before had gone. She felt afraid, frightened of the city, of the whole world outside that window. Cora felt Fletch's manipulative grip tighten. But that grip was her only lifeline too.

A tabby cat slipped out of the shadows and brushed past her skirt, nosing around the heaps of rags and rubbish for anything to eat. Cora took the rag doll out of her bag and pulled her cloak protectively around them both. Despite its squalor, she felt a strange relief to be back in the cellar. Safe, but for how long? There would be a price to pay for her sanctuary, she knew. And whatever Fletch asked her to do in return, Cora couldn't refuse.

She was shaken from her thoughts by voices. The Beam family were making their way out of the cellar.

'I can't leave without my snuff box, Mrs Beam. I swear I put it in my hat.'

'A mouse slept in your hat, Pa. I heard him sneezing all night long,' said Alfie, ducking to avoid a clip round the ear. Mrs Beam shook her head and rolled her eyes. She came over to Cora with a woollen shawl, which she laid in her lap.

'Have this, child, you look like a ghost. It's a good bit of stuff that'll keep you warm,' she said, and hurried off.

Cora wrapped the shawl around her shoulders, touched by Mrs Beam's kindness. Yes, this is better than sleeping on a church portico with drunks and tramps, she thought. The truth is, Cora Parry, you are just like these people, poor and homeless. But they don't sit around feeling sorry for themselves, so neither should you. Cora felt a little of her old courage stir inside. She wasn't beaten yet. If she wanted to be somebody one day, she'd have to learn how to survive, whatever the cost. Being Carrie had helped her feel strong before, maybe it would help her now.

There was a clatter on the steps and Fletch stumbled in with ripped trousers and a bleeding knee. She limped across the room, clutching her side and lowered herself awkwardly onto the mattress.

'Get us a drink, Bird,' she said, wincing with pain.

Cora threw off the shawl and rummaged in the tea chest for the tankard Fletch had given her.

'Get ale, from the Hole,' Fletch wheezed. 'Tell Bess it's for me.'

Cora hurried across the court and entered the tavern nervously. She'd never been inside an inn before. The morning light hardly penetrated its small, dirty windows and a stale smell of ale and pipe smoke hung in the air. A red-faced woman with her sleeves rolled up was strewing handfuls of sawdust from a bucket over the floor. She looked up, squinting at Cora in the doorway. 'We ain't open yet.'

'Are you Bess?' said Cora. 'I need some ale. Please.'

'We don't often hear pretty manners in here,' teased the woman, rubbing the sawdust off her skirt. 'Yes, I'm Bess and who are you, after a drink so early?'

'It's for Fletch.'

'Oh. Give it here.' Bess put down her bucket and took the tankard from Cora's hands.

'You're her new girl, then?' she asked, studying her with curiosity as she held the tankard under the pump and filled it to the brim. Cora smiled awkwardly. The old sailor, Nelson, had asked the same thing. She had an uneasy feeling that 'Fletch's girl' was a well-known role in the rookery. Thanking the barmaid Cora hurried back to the cellar, trying not to spill a drop.

Fletch drank thirstily, draining the tankard to the dregs. 'I got caught in a backyard,' she said, wincing as she lay back and wedged the greatcoat beneath her head. 'The missus came out and I had to scarper quick over the wall, but there was wet leaves on the coal bunker – I slipped and bashed my ribs then I tore my britches going over the top.'

'Do you want me to clean up your knee?' suggested Cora tentatively.

'No, that don't matter, it's the britches.'

'I've got a needle and thread.' Cora took her sewing case from her bag. She felt Fletch's eyes on her.

'I should have brought you with me,' said Fletch as Cora threaded the needle and began to sew. 'If you'd been distracting that woman at the front door I'd have been in and out, quick as a flash.'

As Cora finished the last stitch Fletch twisted to reach for something under the mattress. A blade caught the light and flashed in Fletch's hand. Cora gasped and dropped the needle.

Fletch laughed. 'It's to cut the thread,' she said, offering the knife handle to Cora. 'There's no need to jump. We're friends now, ain't we? I'm going to teach you tricks.'

Cora wondered if that's what Fletch had said to her

other 'girls'. She cut the thread and handed the knife back to Fletch, disturbed to see how lovingly she handled it, weighing it in her hand, as if reluctant to put it away. Church bells interrupted her thoughts, ringing out above the noise of the city's streets.

'Half-past nine,' said Fletch. She got to her feet, flinching with pain. 'You can come with me this time.'

'Where are we going?' asked Cora.

'Don't you know it's Sunday?' Fletch smiled. 'We're going to church.'

13

Cora followed Fletch along the passage out of Farthing Court, full of suspicion. She didn't believe for a minute that Fletch wanted to confess her sins.

She was even more mystified when they arrived at the churchyard just as the congregation was leaving. Fletch led Cora to the window of a draper's shop on the opposite side of the road.

'What are we doing here?' Cora whispered.

'Stay back,' said Fletch, staring at the reflection of the worshippers in the glass. 'First lesson: you can't wait around for chances in life, you got to make opportunities for yourself.' Then she stepped smartly onto the pavement and started to walk off. Cora followed.

Fletch moved furtively, fast then slow, stopping, starting, pausing by a fountain. After a while Cora realised they were following a well-dressed man and his wife who'd been talking to the vicar outside the church.

'Who are those people?' she asked.

'The sort who give their servants the day off on Sunday,' said Fletch. 'I'd put money on it. Once we know where they live we can come back next week, while they're praying for the souls of sinners, and relieve them of some of their worldly goods.' She grinned. 'They'll be feeding us and forgiving us at the same time, see. They'll get their reward in heaven, but I ain't going to wait that long!'

They stalked their victims to a fine town house where the man unlocked the door himself. 'I was right,' said Fletch. 'The servants are out. We'll have an hour undisturbed next Sunday.' It was so simple, thought Cora. Those poor people had no idea they'd been marked by a thief.

'Come on,' said Fletch. 'We don't want to be spotted here.'

When they were a few streets away from the house Fletch slowed to a walk. 'Look like you're idling now, Bird,' she muttered under her breath. 'Keep your ears sharp and your eyes peeled.'

Cora tried to copy Fletch's nonchalant expression as she drifted from one side of the street to the other, crouching by a statue to re-tie her bootlace, then dawdling a few moments later at a market barrow to examine shoe polish and brushes. 'You'll be amazed what you can learn, watching and listening,' Fletch whispered, her eyes darting left and right. 'Broken windows, houses empty all day; people give themselves away with careless talk. See that old woman with a basket?' Cora nodded. 'Wait here.'

Fletch sauntered across the road and followed the old woman for a few steps, then deliberately walked into her, knocking the basket to the ground. Several paper packages and a jar tumbled out. Cora watched Fletch apologise earnestly and put everything back in the basket. She handed it to the woman and they talked for several minutes before the woman clutched Fletch's hand in thanks and continued on her way. Fletch returned to Cora with a sly smile.

'Widow woman, lives on her own down Brewery Street,' she said. 'Husband was a watchmaker. Bet he left her a nice clock in her parlour.'

'How did you find all that out?' asked Cora, horrified to think how easily the old woman had trusted Fletch.

'Careless talk, see. I offered to carry her basket home but she says she only lives close. Turns out I remind her of her boy who went for a sailor, so I asked if her husband was a sailor too.' Cora could imagine how the rest of the conversation went, how easy it would be to follow her and find the house. How distressed the old woman would be to have her clock stolen – and anything else Fletch took a fancy to.

'Once they trust you, all you've got to do is string them along, see, keep them talking,' said Fletch. 'You'll easily fool people with that honest face, Bird. All you need is a good story.'

An honest face and a good story. Is that what she wants from me?

They smelled the sweet scent of apple fritters.

'You hungry?' asked Fletch.

'Yes,' said Cora, with a sigh of resignation. 'Yes, I'm hungry.' *And I'll pay the price.* It was no use fooling herself – Fletch was right, she had no choice.

They found the man frying fritters and Fletch bought them one each. 'I need food to take back to the others,' she said as they tossed the piping hot rings between their hands to cool down. 'Come on, I'll show you how to work the market.'

Cora marvelled at how stealthily Fletch moved from stall to stall, slipping bread rolls and slices of cold meat up her sleeves and then into her pockets, causing a distraction by tripping up a man laden with boxes so she could help herself to three cherry buns.

But she knew it would be her turn next. You're the thief's apprentice now, she told herself. It's this or the workhouse.

'So, let's see what you're made of, Bird,' said Fletch. 'Lunchtime's good pickings.'

Cora stared at her. 'I couldn't,' she stuttered, 'I'm not ready…' The look on Fletch's face silenced her. Cora swallowed hard and followed.

They left the market and turned into a broad, busy street. Fletch pointed to a cobbler's shop. 'That shoemaker has lunch every day with his invalid sister upstairs,' she said. 'From twelve 'til one, while it's quiet, there's only his boy in the shop.'

'What do you want me to do?' Cora was beginning to feel sick.

'It's easy. You just go in and ask for Mr Smith's boots.'

'Who's Mr Smith?'

'I dunno. There's bound to be a customer called Smith, ain't there? While he's in the back room searching, I'll do the rest.'

Cora looked in through the window. Fletch hadn't mentioned that the boy was lame and walked with a crutch.

'He won't be chasing us down the street,' said Fletch coldly.

Cora wondered how many times she'd spied on that shop to be sure of the shoemaker's habits. Her heart was in her throat as Fletch took her by the elbow and walked her across the road.

'Don't think about it, just do it. Smith's boots. Go on.'

Cora's head pounded. What if another customer came in? What was Fletch going to do? Too late, the boy had seen her. Cora stepped inside the shop and walked up to the counter, gripping her cloak to stop herself from trembling.

'I've come for some boots.' Surely her nervous voice would give her away?

'Well, we've got a shop full of boots, 'aven't we, miss?' he replied. His unpleasant tone made it easier.

'They're for Mr Smith. My uncle,' she added.

'Address?' Cora stared at him in panic. She looked over his shoulder at an advertisement for polish.

'Scot Street,' she said, reading the small print at the bottom.

'Never 'eard of it.' The boy shrugged, swung round on his crutch and hobbled into the back room. The moment he was gone Fletch dashed in. She pushed Cora aside, reached across the counter and opened the till. A bell rang as the drawer shot open.

'Hey!' The boy shouted from within.

Cora heard the thud of his stick as Fletch scooped up as much money as she could and stuffed it into her pocket.

'Get out!' Fletch sped past her, spilling coins all over the floor. Cora hesitated, just a pulse. She looked back. The boy hobbled towards her, lurching wildly on his crutch, his ugly mouth cursing, eyes blazing with anger. Someone was shouting upstairs. Cora turned and ran, crashing into a box of stockings as a shoe hurtled through the air after her.

'Two pounds, seven shillings and fourpence halfpenny!' Fletch let the money fall through her fingers and clink into her cap. They'd found refuge two streets away in the wild garden of an empty house. Fletch sat against a tree and Cora lay in the long grass beside her.

'That boy would have killed me with his stick if he'd caught me,' Cora gasped, still trying to steady her heartbeat after pelting down the road.

'You've got to be quicker,' said Fletch, without sympathy.

'Never hang about. You'll soon learn.' She dropped six coins into Cora's hand. 'That feels good, eh? Respectable takings for five minutes' work.'

'I won't do it again,' Cora blurted, not caring what Fletch thought. The adrenalin made her reckless. 'Never, never. I'd rather beg on the street.'

Fletch took the head of a thistle between her finger and thumb and snapped it from its stem. 'Go ahead,' she said. 'But I don't rate your chances much – you ain't pretty or crippled or carrying a child.'

The words were like a slap in the face. Above their heads, a gust of wind rattled through the trees. Cold rain began to fall.

Slowly, resentfully, Cora's fingers closed around the coins.

That night, Cora dreamed that she beat her fists on the door of Walston Workhouse. There was a rattle of locks and the door was opened a crack. She glimpsed a dark figure within.

'Dust to dust, ashes to ashes,' a voice muttered. 'I've been waiting for you.' The door creaked open and a figure stepped out of the shadows. The shoemaker's boy raised his hand, brandishing a knife. He scowled menacingly at Cora. 'I've been waiting to chop off your thieving fingers.'

'No!' Cora turned to run, but, to her horror, she was trapped by an impenetrable wall of shoeboxes.

The boy came close, thumping his crutches on the cobbles.

She spun around. 'You're wrong, it wasn't me.'

'Then who?' He threw down his sticks now and grabbed her hand.

Cora couldn't wrench her hand free. She stared at the fury in his wild eyes. 'Carrie!' she shouted desperately. 'It was her, not me. Carrie did it!'

As the blade of the knife sliced across the palm of her hand she woke, trembling in a cold sweat.

14

'Ouch!'

Fletch grabbed Cora by the wrist as she tried to steal a watch from her pocket for what seemed like the hundredth time. They'd been walking back and forth in the cellar all morning and Cora hadn't even managed to touch the watch without Fletch feeling her pocket twitch.

Fletch had spent three days teaching Cora the tricks of her trade. They'd pinched clothes from a washing line and food from the market. Cora had learned how to pick a lock, and how to fake a faint in the street and cause a stir so Fletch could work the crowd. Most importantly, she'd learned how to make a fast escape.

'Always remember, work out which way to bolt before you make a move,' Fletch told her. Everywhere they went she showed Cora secret routes through back alleys, places to hide, how to become invisible. Cora listened hard and learned fast. She knew her life depended now on not getting caught. But there was one skill she still couldn't master.

'Concentrate!' barked Fletch. 'Make a definite move and be quick.'

'Yes, Fletch.' Cora rubbed her sore wrist. 'It's just that ... I can't ...'

'You said you was as strong as a boy,' Fletch sneered. 'But it's not strength that matters, it's nerve – you need nerve like a boy. Don't snivel.' She smacked Cora sharply across the back of the head. 'If you're not up to it I'll find someone who is.' Fletch picked up her cap and started to walk towards the door.

Cora's head smarted. She was choked with anger. *I hate her. I'll show her I've got nerve.* By the time Fletch reached the bottom of the steps Cora had the watch in her hand.

'Here,' she cried, dangling it from her fingers defiantly.

Fletch spun round. 'That's it!' Her eyes flashed with approval. 'I knew you had it in you!' She snapped up the watch in her hand and put it back in her pocket. 'See, Bird. You've got to get hungry for it, you've got to get mad at the world. When you're mad, you ain't afraid.'

Later, Cora lay awake listening to Fletch murmur in her sleep. Was it anger that made her so fearless? she wondered. What had happened in Fletch's life to make her like this? Cora knew she'd never dare ask. She remembered the triumphant feeling of the watch in her hand and smiled. She'd shown Fletch that she had nerve all right.

Next morning Fletch woke Cora early. 'Come on,' she whispered, shaking Cora by the shoulder. 'Time for work.'

Cora sat up and blinked sleepily. It was hardly light outside. She made out the figure of the dog boy, stumbling through the doorway, his dog traipsing behind. Everyone else in the cellar was still asleep.

Cora laced her boots obediently. She grabbed the shawl Mrs Beam had given her, wrapped it over her cloak and followed Fletch out of the cellar.

They walked in silence for half an hour, out of the slums, through a park and along streets of fine houses, until they came to a broad thoroughfare of grand shops and restaurants which were just opening for business. Cora slowed to gaze at the beautiful clothes and expensive hats in the windows.

'I s'pose you'd like all that fancy stuff?' said Fletch, pulling her along by the sleeve.

Any girl would, thought Cora. Any normal girl. She wondered what Fletch wanted, what she dreamed of.

'There's only one way the likes of you is gonna have a feather in her hat,' said Fletch. 'And that's if you snatch it. That's why we're here.'

'For a hat?' Cora felt stupid as soon as she'd said it.

'No, for a snatch – a purse.'

Cora was alarmed. They hadn't practised stealing a purse.

'It's easy,' said Fletch, seeing the panic in her eyes. She pulled Cora into a side alley. 'Listen. Down the bottom of this alley, on the left, there's a door – looks like it's boarded up but it's not. It leads to steps that take you down to the river. There's a big drain comes out at the bottom; it stinks a bit and might be wet but it's big enough to hide in. We'll meet in there.'

'What have I got to do?' Cora felt sweat on her hands. Fletch pulled a folded newspaper out of her pocket.

'I'll set myself up with the paper round the corner, in front of the coffee house. Next door there's a big department store. I'll keep watch for someone who's loaded up with shopping and carrying a purse. You stand in front of the big window, gazin' at stuff, just like you was. Keep looking, no matter how long, but be ready. As soon as I make a move and knock into somebody, you pick up their purse and run. Don't look back, d'yer hear? No matter who starts shouting, just belt around the corner and get through that door before somebody follows. Got it?'

Cora's throat was so dry she couldn't speak. She nodded.

'Now, you go first,' hissed Fletch. 'Go!'

Cora took a deep breath and walked the few steps to the window of the department store. This is worse than the cobblers, she thought. This time she was the thief. She positioned herself close to the doorway, numb with terror. A few moments later, out of the corner of her eye, she saw Fletch amble along and lean against the wall of the coffee shop. Fletch pulled the paper out from under her arm, tugged her cap down low and studied the news.

The store was already busy. A succession of well-dressed

women arrived in carriages and the doorway quickly became congested with customers passing in and out. Cora lost sight of Fletch. Her mind raced. *Keep calm, just look out for a purse and then run.* A smart woman came up and stood beside her, looking her up and down suspiciously. *Don't flinch.* Cora tipped her head, pretending to consider the cut of a brown jacket on the model in the window. *Grab the purse, just grab it and don't look back.* Get mad, Fletch had said, but that wouldn't make it right.

Suddenly there was a shrill cry and a woman carrying several packages collapsed onto the pavement, flinging the parcels from her arms. A box fell against Cora's knee and crashed to the ground with the sound of breaking glass. Her heart leapt to her throat. She stared at the flailing figure and couldn't move.

'Sorry, Missus!' Fletch's voice cut through Cora's fear. Fletch bent over the woman to help her up and, with a deft kick of her boot heel, sent a silver purse spinning towards Cora's foot. *Do it. Now.* Cora ducked down and grabbed the purse, shoved it inside her cloak and pushed her way out of the gathering crowd. *Don't look back, just run.* Cora skidded on wet leaves as she swung round the corner and pelted down the alley. She found the door at the end and fumbled with the handle. Why wouldn't it move? There was shouting now, men's angry voices in the street. Cora kicked the door. She'd be caught red-handed if she couldn't get out. She kicked again harder and the door budged a few inches. Cora breathed in and squeezed through, grazing her face and snagging her skirt on a nail. With a wrench she tugged it free and pushed the door closed again just as footsteps reached the alley.

'She couldn't have gone down there, it's empty.'

'You fetch the manager, I'll take a look …'

Cora gripped the purse tight and ran on. A set of steep stone steps descended to a dark stairwell. She lifted her skirts and leapt them two at a time. Turning at the bottom she found herself stepping into the mud of the riverbank. The mouth of the drain gaped nearby. Cora flung herself into the dark entrance with a splash.

She slumped inside. Her heart beat like a drum, her heaving breath echoed around the chamber. Where was Fletch? All was quiet outside, she was sure she hadn't been followed, but had Fletch been as lucky? Had somebody seen her kick the purse?

The purse. Cora had been aware of something bulky inside it when she was running. She examined it, stroking the fine satin pouch and silver clasp. Inside, she found paper money, coins and a key, a couple of visiting cards and a gold locket with a broken chain. Cora lifted out the locket.

Just then a pair of seagulls shrieked close by, there was a squelch of mud and Fletch's frame filled the mouth of the drain. She had to bow low to fit inside.

'I'll take that,' she said, pouncing on the locket. 'You done well, Bird.' Her voice boomed around the hideaway. Cora edged in deeper to give her room. 'Pity about the chain, it would have fetched more.' She opened the locket and shook the contents into her hand.

'What's in it?' asked Cora.

'Nothing,' said Fletch dismissively and threw the tiny things into the water. 'Give us the rest. Let's get out of this hole.'

As Cora followed Fletch out, she paused to pick up the little oval photo floating on the dirty water. It was a portrait of a smiling young girl with bright eyes and long ribbons. The other piece of card contained a lock of golden hair, fixed into a paper frame. On the back Cora read 'Darling Elsie May. Three months old.'

'You coming?' Fletch shouted, already picking her way through the mud towards a jetty.

Cora clutched the damp photo and the lock of hair in her hand, filled with guilt and shame. That locket must have been so precious. She imagined the woman's distress at losing it. Wishing there was a way to return the mementos, she trudged after Fletch.

Cora slept restlessly that night. She dreamed that she was running through a dark, empty street. The only light spilled from a shop window and when she reached it she stopped. In the window sat a beautiful woman in a green dress, with pale skin and raven hair, rocking a small child in her arms. It was the woman Cora had seen struggling on the pavement, the woman she had robbed. The child hugged her mother tight and Cora saw she had a paper pinned to her dress with the words, For Sale.

'How much?' said the woman. She stood up and slowly stepped out of the window towards Cora.

'How much for my baby?'

'I don't understand,' stuttered Cora. Rain began fall. Hard and sharp.

'You can sell her, take her.' She held out the child to Cora. 'You take what you want, don't you?'

Cora backed away. She lost her balance and fell onto the pavement. Now the rain was tiny shards of glass, pricking her all over like needles, shattering as they hit the ground. The woman put the child down and produced a long, glass blade.

'Take her. I've been waiting to slice off your thieving little fingers. Thief! Thief!'

Cora cowered in terror. The needles stabbed, the woman's voice bore into her head. 'It wasn't me!'

'Then who?'

The baby had vanished. The woman raised the blade.

'Carrie!' Cora screamed, covering her head with her hands. 'Carrie took it!' She felt the glass slice across her knuckles.

Cora woke with a gasp. What had she become? Shaking feverishly, she reached for Belle. Buried in the rag doll's thick woollen hair was the familiar faint scent of heather from their games on the heath near the village. This was real, this was what she had to remember. I'm not a thief, Belle. I know the difference between right and wrong. But what choice do I have?

Carrie.

The dream had called her name. Cora shut her eyes and brought Carrie to life in her imagination. Not a teacher's companion this time, but a street girl like Fletch, born to the underworld without fear or conscience. Carrie could be the thief's apprentice. Cora felt stronger, braver at the thought. Carrie could protect her from the guilt. Carrie could give her somewhere safe to hide.

Now Fletch saw a change in Cora. There was a quietness, a steadiness in her eye. Fletch watched her protégée carefully. They went to work the crowd milling outside the city zoo, where Cora moved among the people without any show of nerves or hesitation, without any emotion at all. There was no panic in her eye, no trembling hand. She's come to it, thought Fletch with satisfaction. She's mine.

∽ 15 ∽

Anything Fletch stole was taken to a man she called 'the shifter' who lived south of the river. Fletch never took Cora with her, but on her return she counted out a bag of coins and gave Cora a share. Cora had no illusions that this was a fair division. She'd heard the dog boy describe how Fletch cheated at cards and gambled on anything from cockfights to drinking matches. Cora added the money Fletch gave her to the other coins they'd stolen.

'Looks like you've got enough to buy your own bed now,' said Mrs Beam one afternoon, as she watched Cora counting what she'd saved. 'I'll take you to Mould's, the second-hand warehouse.' Cora wanted to spend as little as possible. She chose the cheapest mattress, so worn and thin it looked as though several generations of a large family had used it in turn. But it would be her very own. Like an island in a squalid sea, she'd have her own tiny domain. There was a space for it close to the cellar door, at a distance from Fletch and Marnie, so she arranged herself there and, when no one was looking, hid her spare coins inside a tear in the lining. This would be the beginning of her savings. When I've got enough to pay for a room we'll get out of this filthy cellar and I'll find work teaching somewhere, she told Belle. Then she'd be respectable and independent, sweeping into a sunny room with a book in her hand, her head held high. While Carrie protected Cora, the dream kept her hope alive.

Fletch's trip to the shifter often took a couple of days. Cora suspected this was because Fletch went off gambling as soon as she got the money, but it did leave her time to herself. Time in which she could escape to see Joe. Cora cleaned herself up at the water pump and set off to give him his second reading lesson, trying to come up with a convincing story along the way in case Fletch returned early and found her gone.

'The letters A to M weren't much use to me without the rest,' Joe teased her. 'I thought you weren't coming back. What have you been doing all this time?' Cora smiled at Mr Tally behind the counter as Joe led her into the back of the shop.

'Nothing much,' she said. 'We've got lots of pupils at the moment.' Cora was glad Joe's back was turned so he couldn't see her cheeks flush. What would he think if he knew the truth? Being Carrie couldn't protect her from the guilt of lying.

Joe produced a family Bible and a slate and chalk.

'Look, I found these for us to use. It's a real fancy school book.' He thumbed through the gold-leafed pages in wonder. 'Where do we start?'

'Let's find a good story,' she suggested. Joe's trust made it easy to play the respectable teacher's assistant he thought she was, the person she wanted to be.

Joe learned quickly and laughed easily at his own mistakes. He didn't ask Cora any more questions about herself, and for a happy hour her other life was forgotten.

'Why don't you want your father to know what you're doing?' she asked, when they reached Z for Zachary and Zebadiah at last.

'I don't want him to feel bad that he can't teach me himself,' said Joe. 'He can't read either, see.'

'But he'll have to find out sooner or later.'

Joe hid the book and slate behind the chaise longue. 'I'll surprise him one day, when I've mastered it,' he said. 'Imagine the look on his face when I pick up the paper and read him the news.' Joe jumped up, pleased with himself. 'Now, come and see Pip. Snub locked him up in a parrot cage in the yard this morning for stealing his eye glass – but I reckon he's been a prisoner long enough!'

For the rest of the afternoon Cora and Joe played with Pip in the backyard, teaching him new tricks, until Mr Tally called for help in the shop.

'I need you to look after things for a while, Joe,' he said. 'Snub's gone home sick – it's just a case of the gripes, but he thinks he's dying! I promised to deliver a letter for him to his aunt.'

'I'll be all right here,' said Joe. 'Carrie can help me, can't she, Pa? She's honest, you can trust her.'

Cora suddenly felt awkward. 'No, Joe,' she said. 'I've got to go now too, I'll be needed shortly. But I'll see you very soon.'

'Well, you've got Pip, Joe,' said Mr Tally, following Cora to the door. 'If you get a sudden rush he'll keep them all in order!'

Cora hated leaving the cosiness of the shop to return to Farthing Court. She was determined not to stay away so long again. Soon she'd be able to get a room of her own. Then she'd never have to steal and lie again. It wouldn't be long now, and then she could leave Carrie behind.

Mr Tally came home later that evening in a thoughtful mood. Joe had already locked up the shop and lit the fire in the little room above that served as both parlour and bedroom. His father produced a parcel of fish and chips for supper, but as they ate Joe noticed he was unusually quiet. Joe filled the silence by talking about his new friend and the games they'd played with Pip. When they had finished eating, Mr Tally pushed his empty plate aside and picked up a small painting from the mantelpiece.

'The most important thing you must learn in our business, Joe,' he said, turning the painting over in his hands, 'is how to spot a fake. Everything depends upon it. You must know the tell-tale signs that give the game away. Don't be fooled by appearances.'

Joe wasn't sure what his father was referring to. They both knew that Joe's grandmother had painted the picture.

'But what do we do with a fake, Pa?' he asked, clearing away the fish papers.

'Oh, we handle it all right,' said Mr Tally, 'just like the good stuff. If it's worth faking it's probably worth having. But we must know what it's worth. That's what matters. Fake or genuine, we must know what it's worth to us. Remember that, son.'

Joe noticed a strange, faraway look in his father's eye. Mr Tally put the picture back on the mantelpiece and picked up a small box lying beside it. He sat in his armchair and took a tarnished medal out of the box, then he searched his pockets for a handkerchief and began to polish it. To Joe's dismay he saw his father's eyes well with tears.

Joe stoked the fire and made them both a cup of tea. He sat down at his father's feet. 'Tell me the story, Pa,' he said eagerly. 'Tell me about the storm at sea and Captain Bristow and the shipwreck ...'

Mr Tally sighed and smiled at his son. 'Don't you ever tire of that one?'

'No, Pa,' cried Joe, gazing earnestly at his father's face. 'It's amazing 'cos it's true. I wish I'd seen you sailing that raft with the waves rising up as big as mountains.' His eyes were alight with pride. Mr Tally put his tea cup on the table beside the chair, took off his glasses, and began the tale that Joe had heard a hundred times before.

❦ 16 ❦

In the days that followed, Cora found herself drawn deeper into her strange double life. She worked for Fletch, stealing for her supper, but went to visit Joe as often as she could get away. Fletch regularly left her alone now, sometimes because she took the dog boy or the trolley boy to do a job instead, sometimes she went off mysteriously with Marnie. Often she just disappeared with no explanation. Cora never dared ask what she did or where she went and Fletch seemed content as long as Cora was there when she wanted her. While she remained in that place Fletch owned her. It was the price she paid. Cora learned to play two parts – Carrie the thief, and Carrie the teacher, and she played them well.

In Fletch's absences, Cora tried again to look for work,

keeping well away from the rookery for fear of her finding out. But though Cora cleaned her face at the pump and brushed down her clothes, she was turned away, time and time again.

'We have scores of girls like you asking to wash dishes,' she was told. 'There just aren't enough jobs for all of you.' Cora's dream of teaching became her only hope, but for that she'd have to wait until she'd saved enough money for board and lodgings. Just a little longer, just a few more jobs.

Not long after Cora's return to the cellar she noticed Fletch was growing agitated and unsettled. Fletch talked about a plan, something ambitious.

'If we pull it off you'll be able to fill your lumpy old mattress with silver,' she said, as they walked back to Farthing Court late one night.

'How do you know about that?' Cora was annoyed to hear her hiding place had been discovered. Her savings, her only chance of escape. She kicked out at a lamppost, wishing it was Fletch's shin.

'Don't worry, I haven't touched your little treasure,' said Fletch with a smirk. 'I've got my eye on real money – a big job. It's risky but you'll get your share if you help me. If you can keep your nerve.'

Cora wondered why Fletch even bothered to pretend that she had a choice. They both knew she didn't.

'We'll have to lie low afterwards,' Fletch said. 'Maybe go to the country for a while. I know a place. When things die down I'll come back for Marnie.'

'Why Marnie?' Cora had often noticed Fletch give Marnie special attention. But, as usual, she didn't answer.

'You're going to keep watch,' Fletch told her. 'I need you to be lookout and help me carry the stuff – that's all. I'll do the rest.' It sounded suspiciously easy. But then why was Fletch so restless?

That night Cora woke to a hand being clapped over her mouth. 'Ssh!' Fletch shoved a thin bundle tied with string into Cora's hands. 'Hide this under your bed, you'll need it tomorrow night. Don't breathe a word.'

Cora nodded. With silent horror she felt a blade inside the bundle. It frightened her. It didn't feel like the kitchen knife Fletch had given her to cut the thread – this was a long, slender blade, not a tool but a weapon. Accepting it felt like taking some dreadful oath, acknowledging that she'd be prepared to use it. Cora stuffed the knife under her mattress, but she couldn't go back to sleep. She lay, staring into the darkness. The shoemaker's boy stepped out of her dream, taunting her with the blade in his hand. It would be dangerous to refuse Fletch.

Cora waited until they were sitting in the tavern with their breakfast bread next morning, surrounded by other people. She hoped she'd be safe from Fletch's temper there. Remember, she told herself, you're Carrie. You're nobody's 'girl'.

'Fletch,' she said, keeping her voice low, 'I'm not coming with you tonight. I won't come, not with knives.'

Fletch chewed her crust and glowered darkly. 'You'll do as you're told, Bird,' she said. Her hand shot beneath the table and gripped Cora's wrist. She jabbed her thumb into the palm of Cora's hand. 'Don't you find five fingers is useful?' she growled under her breath. 'It'd be a pity to break one, eh?' Cora tried to twist her hand away but Fletch held it tight. 'Now, you're not going to let me down, are you?'

'I won't do it!' Cora cried. She wrenched her hand free with a jerk, knocking the table and spilling Fletch's ale all over her breeches. There was no going back now. She looked at Fletch's thunderous face in terror. 'I don't care what you do, I won't go through with it and you can't make me!'

Fletch flexed her fingers, and for a moment Cora thought she might take out a knife there and then. The other customers fell silent. Fletch grabbed Cora by the sleeve and pulled her outside. She pushed her roughly up against the tavern wall. 'I can make you do anything I want, Bird. If you don't want my mark on that pretty face of yours, you'll remember that.' She threw Cora to the ground. 'I've got to talk to Marnie. You be here and ready when I get back, or I'll find you, Bird, just like I found you before. Only next time you'll wish I hadn't!'

Fletch's eyes burned like a brand. I own you, they warned. Don't you dare forget it.

❧ 17 ❧

As soon as Fletch had gone, Cora got up, rubbing her smarting wrist, and stumbled into the cellar. She grabbed the knife from under her mattress and hurried away from the Rookery. All she could think about was getting rid of it. She took any street, walking on and on until the rhythm of her footsteps calmed her throbbing head. When she came to a neglected graveyard with an open gate, she slipped inside. The hedges around the graveyard were overgrown with brambles. Cora chose a dark corner, fell to her knees and dug with her hands among the roots. She buried the knife as deep as she could and covered it with earth. With the knife out of sight she sat back in the long grass and breathed easy. But she couldn't bury Fletch's threat. Cora clasped her dirty hand to her cheek. Fletch really would cut her if she caught her now. Something frightening had happened to her at the tavern. Cora had heard about Fletch's violent outbursts but she'd never seen her like that before. Cora knew nothing would protect her if they ever met again. There was no going back to Farthing Court now.

She left the graveyard deep in thought. *All I have to do is keep out of the way and hope that Fletch still does this job tonight without me and leaves town.* Cora knew she had to stay as far away as possible from Farthing Court. But she was afraid of straying too far from Joe and his father. The pawnbroker's shop was the only place in London where she felt safe, where she'd begun to feel that she belonged.

A warning shout from the road made her jump back just in time to avoid a black carriage that was charging along at a pace. Out of the corner of her eye she thought she saw the head of a red snake flash past. Who had spoken to her about red serpents? The woman at the workhouse. Walston Workhouse. There it was again, finding a way into her mind when she was weak and afraid. But she wouldn't be drawn back now. She was Carrie, and Carrie knew how to survive on the street. Fletch had taught her that, at least.

Cora found herself in the district of theatres and music halls. The bright posters of the actors in fabulous costumes and dramatic poses cheered her. Some of the actors were arriving for afternoon performances and greeted each other at the stage door. How strange, she thought, stopping to watch and listen. They're about to perform in this grand theatre and make the audience laugh and cry, but they're really just ordinary people, complaining about the traffic and worrying about the weather. Why did she feel disappointed? Perhaps it wasn't so extraordinary to play a part after all. She'd learned how to behave like a schoolmaster's daughter, but it had always been a game of pretend. Being Martha's servant had only been bearable because she'd known inside she was somebody else, somebody better. *Now I've become exactly what Fletch wanted.* Cora wished she could walk away from the parts she played, like those actors at the end of the day, and just be herself. But who was Cora Parry? If she knew more about her past, about her mother, maybe she'd understand. The only link was Walston, the place she had sworn never to enter. That, and her mother's box.

Cora realised with a shock that her bag was still in the cellar. When Fletch had left her outside the tavern that morning she'd been so shaken that she'd just grabbed the knife and run. She hadn't even brought the money she'd saved. Cora paced back and forth in front of the theatre. She had to get her things. She needed that money; she'd risked her neck for it. But it was too dangerous to go back now. There was nothing to do but wait until tomorrow, and hope that Fletch had gone ahead alone with her plan, and left the city.

Later that evening Cora returned to the same church where she'd slept once before. This time she had no intention of repeating her cold, uncomfortable night among the tramps and drunkards on the portico. She had learned to be Carrie now, and Fletch's clever tricks would serve her well. She walked around the building and scrambled over a wall at the back. A little window there had been left ajar for so long that ivy had grown inside the frame and it was easy to work loose. She prised it open and climbed into one of the vestry rooms. It was no problem now for her to pick the lock of the largest cupboard where she found several voluminous priests' vestments. She wrapped herself in a purple robe, climbed into the cupboard and curled up. Despite breaking in to a church, her sleep that night was not disturbed by a twitch of guilt. Carrie the thief, the intruder, never dreamed.

Cora returned to Farthing Court next morning. She crept down the cellar steps and peered through a hole in the papered window, but could see little. Listening for the sound of Fletch's voice, she peeped nervously around the door.

Two figures sat on Fletch's bed. Cora froze. Then she saw it was the Russian woman, with her arms around Marnie's shoulders. Marnie was weeping, tears streaming down her cheeks. Cora could just make out the tiny bird's wing trembling in her cupped hands.

'What's wrong?' Cora stepped inside and went to kneel beside them, forgetting all caution. Had something dreadful happened? The Russian woman gave Cora a bewildered shrug.

'Marnie's little princess all gone.' Marnie sighed deeply and more tears rolled down her face. 'All gone from Marnie.'

At that moment, Mr Griddle, the long-song seller, came in with his stick and suitcase. 'She's heard, then,' he said, taking off his tall hat. 'Fletch was arrested last night. Caught red-handed at a big house by the park.'

Cora sat back in shock. Fletch had gone through with her job alone, then. 'Where is she now?'

'She'll be up before the judge, I expect,' said Mr Griddle, shaking his head gloomily. 'They won't hang about with this case. She cut someone with a knife. Apparently the owner came home unexpectedly and went for her. Of all people, it turned out to be the magistrate.'

Cora was horrified. Had Fletch known whose house she was robbing?

'Who's going to give Marnie her silver and gold?' Marnie moaned miserably. 'Silver bells and cockleshells ...'

'Well, we'll look after you now,' said Mr Griddle gently. 'She'll find it hard,' he murmured to Cora. 'Fletch was her daughter, after all.'

Cora stared at him in astonishment.

The mood in the cellar was lively when everyone returned that evening. Cora had never seen them so animated. The boy with the trolley took great pleasure in the news that Fletch had gone.

'I hope she swings,' he said. 'I've seen her cut a man over dice – vicious she was and I swear she enjoyed doing it too.'

'Give over,' said the dog boy. 'She's no worse than most of those rookery women. She had to be tough to keep the wrong sort out of here.'

'I'm sorry she didn't finish him off,' said Mordecai, who had a hatred of the law. 'The fewer magistrates, the better!'

'Who's going to look after the sick ones now?' muttered his wife. 'She never let them down.'

Cora didn't know what to think. She'd hated Fletch. Fletch had stolen from her and threatened her with violence. She'd bullied her and forced her into a life she hadn't wanted. *But I'd be in the workhouse for sure if it wasn't for her.* Fletch had taught her how to survive. Cora looked at Marnie. She had silently moved her bags onto Fletch's bed and was sitting there, mournfully, like a dog waiting for its owner to come home. It was hard to believe that poor Marnie, who shuffled about the streets collecting leaves, was Fletch's mother. Cora wondered how she'd feel if her own mother was as simple as a child, if she'd had to see her stooped so low. Maybe that explained the terrible anger, the fierce sense of injustice that seemed to burn in Fletch's heart.

Cora noticed the baby's mother, Nellie, sobbing quietly as she sat unravelling the wool from an old shawl. Cora went to sit beside her and took up the wool to wind.

The baby watched them sleepily from his basket.

'What's the matter?' asked Cora, surprised at her sadness, in contrast with the lively mood of the rest of the room's inhabitants.

'Just hungry, Miss.' Nellie sniffed her tears away. For the first time Cora realised the girl was much younger than she'd thought. An idea began to form in her mind.

'Did Fletch bring you food every day?' she asked.

'Fletch always give us something,' said Nellie, tugging wearily at the stubborn stitches of the shawl. 'I have to feed the littl'un too, see. Now she's gone I s'pose I'll have to get us to the workhouse.'

'Oh no!' cried Cora. 'You mustn't do that!' She dropped the wool and grasped Nellie's hands. She couldn't let Nellie suffer the same fate as her own mother, or even worse, risk being smuggled out at dead of night to suffer some sinister fate 'What if I could bring you food,' she said, 'just like Fletch did?'

Nellie's face crumpled with tears again. 'Oh, Miss, would you really? Thank you,' she cried, 'thank you!' She hugged Cora tight.

Cora felt Nellie's arms around her, clinging desperately and suddenly realised the enormity of what she'd just promised. What was she doing? Fletch's oppressive reign was over, she was free to walk away, to make a new life, a life where she'd never have to lie or steal again. But her heart ached at the touch of Nellie's frail body, her grateful tears. Cora looked at the helpless baby. If there had been somebody to help her own mother, maybe she'd never have died alone in the workhouse.

'Don't worry,' said Cora. 'I'll look after you now.'

And what about the others who relied on Fletch? The invalid, Signor Peretti, groaned restlessly in his sleep nearby, while Marnie, sitting beside him, vacantly plaited wisps of her long grey hair. Cora touched the baby's hand and he clasped her thumb tight. *I could make a difference. I could do something good here.* She kissed the tiny curled fingers. Maybe there *was* a better feeling than coins in her hand.

Cora's mind raced with new plans, new hope. Fletch had taken all the money hidden in her mattress. She was left with nothing, no money to buy food for Nellie and the others, no savings. At least Fletch hadn't bothered with her bag. She opened it and lifted out Belle.

There wasn't much else left to pawn – a spare pair of stockings, the sewing case and her mother's box. She'd never part with that. Then there was the red dress she'd been given. Cora fingered the embroidered collar. She'd been afraid to get it out and wear it. The dress had seemed too striking, too beautiful to be soiled in the dirty cellar or torn scrambling over walls after Fletch. She'd been saving it for when things got better and she had a room of her own, a respectable job. That seemed foolish now. It ought to fetch something at the pawnbroker's, but it didn't solve her problem.

The rag doll's wide eyes stared back at her, unblinking. Cora thought about everything Fletch had taught her, all her skills and knowledge, her scams and tricks. She thought about being Carrie, how it had enabled her to conquer her fear and made her strong. A familiar voice whispered inside her head and she knew exactly what she had to do.

❧ 18 ❧

A girl in a black cloak disappears into a passage and emerges moments later onto the street; a gust of wind ruffles her hem to reveal a flash of red beneath. Her eyes dart left and right, sharp as a fox, and she slips away into the morning mist.

Carrie walks away from her conscience as though she has stepped out of her skin. She stalks the streets, looking for opportunity. She finds windows ajar, a ruined warehouse with its back door kicked in, a delivery wagon left unattended, while its driver warms himself beside a night watchman's brazier. She watches a shopkeeper open his door with a yawn, then disappear into his back room to put the kettle on – and, two doors away, an empty alley for a swift escape.

This city owes me, she thinks, just like all the others it has buried and forgotten in filthy cellars. It owes us what we need to survive.

Later that morning, Carrie crosses a busy street as a dogfight suddenly erupts in the path of an oncoming carriage. The carriage horse takes fright and rears wildly. Screams and shouts ring out in alarm as the driver struggles to control the horse and the carriage lurches violently. Carrie jumps into a doorway just in time as luggage piled high on the roof breaks free of its lashes and crashes to the ground. The terrified horse pulls away. The carriage hits a fishmonger's cart and topples over onto its side, flinging the coachman to the pavement. Passers-by flock to pull the passengers and driver from the wreckage, but the horse is trying to break free from its twisted harness. It panics, stamping and whinnying, eyes rolling, preventing anyone from getting close.

Carrie holds back. She has caught sight of a trunk that has fallen against the kerb and broken apart. A lady's belongings are strewn amongst the debris of splintered tubs and spilled fish. Something gold glints under a slithering heap of mackerel. A clock, right there within her reach. She snatches it up and stuffs it under her cloak, pausing to grab a jacket and a pair of boots as well, then without looking back she scrambles round the corner and away.

Carrie pauses in the shadows of Farthing Court, heart pounding fast. Unobserved, she walks swiftly towards the railing of the cellar stairs and then beyond, slipping around the corner into a passage between that house and its empty neighbour. No footsteps following, she slumps against the wall and lets herself breathe easy. With the breath comes elation. Here's treasure and it almost fell at my feet, she laughs to herself. Whoever this

belonged to will still eat tonight; they won't sleep in a cellar.
But the clock has to be hidden a while, just to be safe. She takes off
the red dress that she's been wearing over her own, folds it up and
puts it in a sack, her guilt wrapped tightly within. The clock goes
in after. At the end of the passage is a broken barrel. She lowers
the sack inside.

Cora stepped out from between the houses and descended
the cellar steps, feeling lighter and happier than she'd done
in a long time.

The jacket and boots were too small for Nellie, but
they were just the right size for the Russian woman, who
thanked her gratefully.

It had been a while since Cora had visited Joe. Now
her time was her own she'd be able to see him whenever
she wanted. She just had to take care; her precious
new freedom would be short-lived if she was careless
and got caught like Fletch.

Before she could go to the pawn shop she went to clean
herself up. Carrie, the teacher's assistant, had to play her
part well. She went to the tavern yard where there was

a tub and tap for washing. Bess the barmaid came out, eager for a chat. Since their first meeting, Cora had come to know her as a compulsive busybody and gossip.

Bess sat on the step, slipped off her shoes and rubbed her feet. 'Did you hear about the accident on Sparrow Row yesterday? A carriage got into a terrible crash with Henry Hake's barrow and broke two wheels.'

Cora's heart missed a beat. She hid her face in the rag Bess left out for a towel.

'Anyway,' continued Bess, 'the poor lady what was inside took a bang to the head and has completely lost her memory! The coachman, he broke his leg, well, he remembers picking her up from 'ampstead 'eath but she was travelling on from somewhere else – and nobody knows who she is! Imagine – all your life gone from your head. Mind you, for most round here it'd be a blessing!'

'Hopefully her memory will come back,' said Cora, heaving the empty water tub back to its place against the wall. The sudden revelation had caught her off guard.

'The poor woman's memory might come back but her belongings won't!' said Bess. 'Half her things were took while they pulled her free. Who'd steal from a woman what doesn't know who she is?'

'Did anyone see who took them?' Cora picked at a fern growing out of the damp wall, pretending to be only half interested.

'Somebody saw a girl run off with her arms full of stuff.' Cora froze. 'A girl in a black cloak and a scarlet dress.'

Her heart thumped, sweat prickled down her back. She

knew she had to say something, do something to protect herself.

'I've seen that girl,' she said, trying to stay calm. 'A girl in a scarlet dress. Selling matches, outside the theatres. It must have been her.'

'Well, who can make a living selling matches? Others are bound to get bolder now that Fletch is out of the way,' said Bess. 'Have you heard? She's inside for a long time. The magistrate said transportation or the rope was too good for her. He wants her locked up in prison, so she suffers the worst for what she done. At least Marnie can visit her, I s'pose.' There was a crash in the kitchen. Somebody cursed and shouted for Bess. With a groan, she put on her shoes and shuffled off.

Cora sighed with relief. If anyone had recognised her she would have known about it by now. Still, it was close. If she was going to stay here she needed to distance herself from Carrie. She needed to build up an alibi and avoid suspicion. Bess and her gossip would be useful.

Joe seemed happy to see Cora when she arrived at the pawnshop, but she noticed at once that he was subdued.

'Penny for your thoughts,' she said, as they followed Pip into the store room.

Joe fetched his slate and chalk from the shelf. 'It's my

pa,' he sighed, slumping onto the chaise longue. 'I'm sure there's something wrong with him.'

'Is he sick?' Cora sat down beside him and plumped up the bolsters.

'No. He's eating all right. I can't work it out. He's just so quiet these days, as if his mind is far away, and he goes out without saying where. It's not like him at all.' Cora remembered Elijah going out for walks alone, but she was sure it had been to escape Martha's nagging.

'Maybe he just wants time to think. It always seems to be so busy in the shop.'

'Well, whatever he's thinking about, he don't tell me,' said Joe. 'He's hiding something. I hate secrets – they shut people out.'

Cora pursed her lips. She took the slate from his hands and started to write the letters of the alphabet, pressing the stick of chalk so hard that it broke with a snap and skidded across the board.

'How stupid, look, what a mess,' she flustered, brushing the chalk dust from her skirt. Joe watched. He'd never noticed the filthy, frayed hem of her skirt or her worn cuffs before.

'Where do you live, Carrie?' he asked, picking up the chalks.

'Oh …' She hesitated. Every time he used that name he forced her to spin another lie. 'I live near the park.' She started writing again to avoid his eye. 'One of those tall houses. I've got a room at the top.'

'Where do you go when you're not working?' He looked at her worn boots, split at the seams.

'Walking,' she shrugged, filling out the curves of the letter S. 'Just walking round the park.'

Joe saw frayed hems and cuffs every day in that place and he knew they didn't come from nice houses by the park. He remembered what his father had said about spotting a fake. Had it been a warning? What matters is what it's worth to you, he'd said. Well, friendship's worth a story, Joe thought to himself, as Cora handed him the alphabet to finish, but he didn't like secrets. He'd grown up in a world where everything had its label, its name and value clearly marked. What were they hiding, his pa and this girl? And why were they hiding secrets from him?

'There's something odd about Carrie, Pa,' said Joe, when his father returned that evening. 'Something doesn't add up.'

'There's not a soul in this world without troubles, son,' said Mr Tally. 'We all just need someone to talk to.' He pulled an orange out of his pocket and tossed it to Joe, who caught the unexpected gift with delight. Joe held the fragrant fruit to his nose.

'It ain't my birthday,' he laughed.

'Life is full of surprises!' His father winked. Joe began to peel it at once.

'I don't think Carrie tells me the truth, Pa,' he continued, dropping the peelings in his lap. 'She says she's a teacher's companion but her clothes don't look respectable enough. I'm sure it's not true. And what about all those things she brings to the shop? I can't work it out and she never likes me asking. Can't we help her somehow? Could she share our supper next time she comes?' He pulled the orange apart and popped a segment of orange into his mouth.

Mr Tally watched the juice sparkle on his son's lips and smiled. 'You're a kind boy, Joe,' he said. 'But we can't do that. You know we only just manage on what we have. It wouldn't be fair to bring her into our family, to give her hope of more and then have to turn her away another time when there's nothing in the pot.'

'But you've got your navy pension, Pa,' said Joe. 'We always have that, don't we?'

'Yes, son,' sighed Mr Tally. He gave Joe a reassuring nod. 'Nothing changes there.'

❦ 19 ❦

A week after the carriage crash on Sparrow Row, Cora decided it was safe to pawn the clock. I'll take it in when Joe isn't there so he can't ask any awkward questions, she thought. Snub won't care where anything comes from as long as he gets his money. Cora knew that Joe and his father often went out on Monday mornings when the shop was quiet. Sure enough, when she got to Mite Street, Snub was alone, leaning on the counter reading a newspaper.

'Joseph is out,' he said, barely raising his eyes from the paper.

'I've come to bring this.' Cora lifted the clock out of her bag and Snub paid attention at once. He reached for his eyeglass.

'Hmm, not bad,' he said, trying to disguise any hint of real worth. As he examined the case, a headline in the newspaper caught Cora's eye. 'Three more young women disappear from Walston Workhouse.'

'These scratches reduce the value, of course,' said Snub dismissively. 'It's worth three shillings, not a penny more.' He took a ticket from the box. 'What name?'

'Carrie.'

'Address?'

'Just Carrie.'

Snub gave her a disapproving look and went off to fetch some wrapping to protect the clock. Cora read on. 'Lottie Parker, a laundress returning home late, reported seeing a carriage leave the workhouse on the night the women disappeared. Staff strongly denied anyone visited that evening. Conditions in Walston are considered some of the harshest in the country and the trustees ...'

The workhouse again. It never let her forget.

Snub thumped a pile of wrapping cloths down on the paper. 'Just keeping informed about some of our customers,' he said. 'It's useful to know which ones have moved address to Newgate Gaol this week.'

Cora walked away from the pawnbroker's thinking about the report of the disappearing girls. She remembered the old woman outside Walston and her story of the Devil's coach. Why would anybody take them off in secret, in the middle of the night? She shuddered to think that she, or Nellie, might have been one of them. Carrie would make sure that neither of them suffered that fate.

Cora stopped outside the window of a junk shop, and decided to go in and take a look. It felt good to have money in her pocket, even if she wasn't going to spend it here. She edged her way among the stacks of chairs and wardrobes, idly picking up whatever small thing took her fancy. The collection of worn and tattered household objects reminded her a little of the pawnbroker's, but the careless way they were crammed together had none of the homeliness of Mr Tally's shop. She stopped in front of a three-sided dressing table mirror. There, before her, was her full face and profiles left and right: three images, each one part of the same, but different. She turned a little, this way and that; everything changed. The face was familiar, but each profile showed aspects of herself she hadn't seen before, the angle of her jaw, the curve of her brow, two tiny freckles on her left ear. Three girls. Here we are, she thought: Elijah's little Cora, Joe's friend, Carrie the thief. What would her mother think if she could see her now? She'd be ashamed, answered a voice inside her head. But I'm all alone, Cora said silently. I have to look after myself. She pushed the stiff side mirrors closed and flicked their tiny catch shut.

'You were right about that match girl,' said Bess, when Cora was in the tavern one morning, a week later, for breakfast. 'Billy Moses, the baker's boy, saw her hanging about the market the other day. He reckons she's a regular little thief. Took off with half a dozen Chelsea buns last Tuesday. Not that he minds, he's on the take like everyone else. But I told him who she was.'

Cora smiled to herself. Good old Bess. The thief in the red dress had already joined a cast of local characters in her mind. Every time Carrie's name was spoken, she would live more clearly, called into being from a whisper of words. Carrie became more confident day by day and Cora more at ease with her double life. She pawned everything that Carrie stole and, with the money she made, managed to buy enough food to share each day, just as Fletch had done.

Like the actors Cora had seen outside the theatre, she remained untouched by the part she played. When the red dress was folded away and hidden in the yard, Carrie's guilt was hidden with it. Nobody noticed her coming and going. Nobody noticed anything at all. Or so she thought.

Joe was not so unobservant.

'He's skulking about upstairs, says he's ill,' said Snub, one Thursday morning when Cora came to give Joe a lesson. 'First the father disappearing off, now the son,' he grumbled. 'There'll be plenty of others who'll take Mr Tally's position. I shall be speaking to my aunt, you can tell him that. There'll be a riot if I'm left on my own in a rush again.'

Cora found Joe in the parlour upstairs, sitting wrapped in a blanket. She saw straightaway from his red eyes and the handkerchief clutched to his nose that he had a bad cold. The room was chilly and Pip's tail swung out from underneath the blanket.

'Are you ill? Shall I light the fire?' she asked, looking at the cold hearth.

'There's no wood,' said Joe gloomily.

'Where's your father?'

'Gone out again. He said he wouldn't be long, but he always says that.'

'I'll fetch you some hot coffee, then.'

'Don't bother,' said Joe. 'Just leave me alone.' He reached for a woollen hat on the table and pulled it over his head. Cora had never seen Joe in a bad mood before. Was it just the cold that made him so short with her?

'Let me do something to help,' she said. 'I'm your friend.'

'Are you?' He stared hard at her. 'How do I know who you are? Look at you ...'

Cora looked down at her stained dress, her grubby shawl and worn boots, the plain evidence of two months on the streets, living in a dirty cellar – the tattered grey plumage of a rookery bird.

'You're not a teacher's companion, are you?' said Joe, looking at her accusingly. 'You never was. And where d'you get all those things you bring Snub? Did you think I wouldn't notice your name on them? Why do you come to him and not me?'

How could Cora answer him? How to unravel the knot of lies she'd told? *It's not me, it's Carrie.* But even Carrie was not the person Joe thought she was.

'You've never been honest with me, have you?' Joe

continued. 'I don't know anything about you, Carrie. I bet that isn't even your real name.'

'Don't ask me, Joe,' said Cora weakly. 'I can't tell you who I am. My life, it isn't like yours ... I don't have a family. I have to look after myself. Please don't spoil it. Can't we just be friends without asking questions?' Pip pushed his way out of Joe's blanket and crept over to Cora.

'You've spoilt it yourself, you've spoilt everything!' Joe cried.

'What do you mean?'

'If you hadn't come here things would have gone on the same as always. Me and Pa, we were happy just how we was.' Joe sniffed and wiped his eyes with his sleeve.

'But what have I done?' Cora was confused. 'What do you mean?'

'Reading!' he snapped. 'If you hadn't taught me to read everything would have stayed like it always was. I wish I'd never seen a book. Just go away and leave me alone.'

'But you asked me, Joe,' she said. 'You wanted to read yourself.'

Joe buried his face in his hands. 'I'm sorry.' With a frustrated sigh, he sank back into his chair and pulled the blanket around his shoulders. 'I didn't mean to be horrible.' He fumbled in his pocket and produced a bag of humbugs, which he held out to Cora as a peace offering. 'It's just that things are all wrong. I don't know who to believe or what to think.' Joe reached out for the medal box and handed it to Cora.

She stroked the golden anchor on the lid. 'Is it from the navy?'

Joe nodded. Cora opened the box. Pip's tiny fingers darted inside to grab the medal, but she took it from him.

'Your pa must have been a real hero to get a medal. See, you're lucky – I don't even know who my father was. Has he told you how he got it?'

'Oh yes,' said Joe. 'He's told me a hundred times – how the ship went down and he saved the captain from drowning. I've grown up knowing that crew like they were my own relations.' His face hardened as he turned over the medal in her hand. Some words were engraved on the back.

'I've never been able to read it before, but now I can.' Slowly he spelt out the words aloud. Patrick O'Leary.

'It's an Irish name,' said Cora, without thinking.

'That may be,' said Joe. 'But it ain't the name of my father.'

❧ 20 ❧

Cora worried about Joe after she left. She had tried to convince him that his father was sure to have a good explanation about the medal, but Joe couldn't be lifted from his black mood. If only she didn't have to pretend to him too. Carrie had once been nothing more than a slip of the tongue, but now Cora needed her. She could never be unspoken.

Joe's angry outburst had made her cautious. Cora knew that she couldn't keep bringing stolen things to Snub. He'd seemed prepared to take anything from her at first, but now she noticed that he, like Joe, had started asking awkward questions. Snub began to refuse things, even good things. If she could find somewhere else to sell them, it would be one less secret to keep from Joe. Cora remembered Fletch and 'the shifter'. It was time to find somebody who wouldn't ask questions.

'Who'll buy this from me then, if you won't?' Cora asked a few days later, when Snub refused to take a silver caddy spoon she had stolen from a tea merchant's warehouse.

Snub shrugged dismissively. 'I wouldn't know that sort of person,' he said quietly, even though there was nobody else in the shop. Cora didn't move. She'd been around thieves and liars long enough to know he wasn't telling her the truth.

'Maybe you know somebody who *does* know?' Snub saw a stubborn light in Cora's eye, a dangerous light. Suddenly he wanted to be rid of her.

'Ask at the wharf, at The Anchor Inn,' he whispered. 'And don't bring anything here again.' With that he turned abruptly on his heel and disappeared into the store room.

Carrie waits a couple of days, until she has more than a silver spoon to sell, before she goes in search of The Anchor Inn. Late in the evening she makes her way down to the river. Along with the spoon, the large pockets she has sewn inside her cloak carry a parcel of fine lace stolen from a haberdasher's shop, a bracelet dropped outside the opera house and a pocket watch taken late at night from a man lying unconscious in an alley.

Down at the wharf, cramped dingy buildings and warehouses crouch along the foreshore, swarming with people. Brawny women with painted faces loll about, arm in arm with swarthy sailors, some dance in high spirits to a fiddle and accordion; bargees and gangs of working men sit drinking and smoking as they stare out at the boats anchored on the river; energetic laughter and music spills from every doorway. Carrie is captivated. The roofs and spires rise above the wharf, but it turns its back on the business of the city and all its eyes gaze seaward, as if its dreams and allegiance lie wherever the water flows.

People sit playing cards and dice on the wharf-side in front of The Anchor Inn. Carrie hangs back, reading the scene, watching for an opportunity. A serving boy shares a joke with some of his customers. When he comes to collect tankards left on the wall she approaches him.

'Can you help me?' she whispers. 'I have things to sell. Is there somebody here who'll buy?'

The boy looks her up and down. 'You want Skelly.' He tips his head for her to follow.

Carrie enters the crowded tavern and is hit by the stench of sweat and ale, the deafening noise of coarse language and laughter. Shiny, dirty faces grin at her, tough-looking men etched with tattoos, toothless, wizened sailors sucking on clay pipes, voluptuous women. Everyone is tense, edgy, alert for trouble. Carrie pushes through after the boy, face cast down, watching all from beneath her lashes. They stop before a door at the back of the room. The boy knocks three times and it opens a crack.

'Somebody for Skelly,' says the boy in a low voice. The dark figure within nods and Carrie is ushered into a smoke-filled room where a dozen men sit around a table, playing cards. For a second they fall silent and stare. She sees at once that these are not like the wharf men outside, quenching their thirst after a day's labour.

They have a skulking, weaselly look about them. Carrie steadies herself and raises her chin a little. To her relief they turn back to their game, all except a thin man with long, black hair and a scar across his cheek. He studies Carrie and she meets his gaze.

'You playing, Skelly?' grunts a man with the pack in his hand.

Skelly takes a look at his cards. 'Ah, you're a swindling nest of vipers,' he snarls. He casts his cards down on the table, kicks back his chair and rises to his feet. 'And where are your manners with a young lady in the room?' He grins and bows and Carrie notices a glint of gold among his rotten teeth. But she doesn't want to reveal her business in front of them. Skelly takes up a candlestick and beckons to her to follow him into a small side room.

'What can I do for you, then, Miss?' he asks as he offers her a chair at a card table and places the candle between them. 'Your face ain't familiar to me.'

'I've got some things to sell,' says Carrie. Adrenalin surges through her blood, sings in her ears. 'They told me you buy stuff, no questions asked.'

'Well now, who told you that?'

'They said no questions asked.' Carrie stares steadily through the candlelight. Keep calm, keep control of yourself.

Skelly scratches his chin and considers her for a moment, then he smiles. 'Show me your treasures, girl.'

Carrie empties her pockets, laying everything out on the table. Skelly gives it all much attention. It only takes him a moment to price the trinkets she's brought, but a moment longer to slyly assess Carrie herself. She waits, giving nothing away. When Skelly has examined it all he offers a price.

'It's a generous price for no questions asked,' he assures her. Carrie hesitates, silently debating, playing his game.

'I'll take it,' she says and he shakes her hand on their agreement. Thieves' manners, she notes. Watch and learn.

'Bring all you have next time, my girl. Nothing's too small.' He lets her out onto the street by a side door. 'There's plenty a sailor boy looking for trinkets to take home.'

When he has withdrawn inside, Carrie collapses against the wall. Her heart races with excitement.

ᘒᔕ 21 ᔕᘒ

While life was easier for Cora now, Joe's spirits seemed permanently low. She made time to see him whenever she could, but although she persuaded him to continue with his lessons he was often uninterested and never played with Pip.

In an attempt to cheer him up one morning, Cora took him a present. 'It's a book of silver hallmarks, see. It's a bit dog-eared but it'll help you with your studies.' Joe took it from her and looked over the pages filled with pictures of tiny shields and stamps, maker's names and dates.

'Where d'you get this?' he asked. Cora's heart sank. He was in a bad mood again.

'I bought it, at the flea market. Don't you like it? When you've got your own shop, you'll need to know all this off by heart.'

Joe put the book down despondently.

'There isn't going to be a shop,' he said. 'It was a stupid dream.'

'What's happened? Why are you talking like this?'

'Snub's got a new man in to help,' said Joe. 'He said he's going to see his aunt and complain about Pa being absent so often. He wants to get us kicked out.'

'Oh, Joe!' said Cora. 'Have you told your father?'

Joe nodded. 'He just said I shouldn't worry and that everything would be all right. It's as if he don't care. He don't care about this place, or me, or what'll happen to us. And I know what'll happen – we'll be out on the street. We haven't got anywhere else to go.'

'What about the medal? Did you ask him about that?'

'No,' said Joe, with a frown. 'I didn't ask him and I don't want to know. It's like he's fading away, right in front of my eyes.'

Cora didn't know what to say. She tried to change the subject.

'I got a new dress, Joe. Do you like it?' He looked at it with suspicion.

'How did you pay for that, then?'

Cora sighed with frustration. She was trying to be nice, why was he turning on her? 'It was a present,' she said fiercely. 'A present from a friend who doesn't ask questions!' She wouldn't let him make her feel guilty. *Carrie takes care of things so I can be here, so I can be his friend. He doesn't realise how difficult it is.* 'Why do you care so much? Why can't you trust me?'

'You and Pa can do what you like,' said Joe. 'But what's

so secret that you can't talk about it to me?'

'I don't need you to be my conscience,' Cora snapped.

Joe picked up an old ticket from the shelf beside him and tore it silently into tiny pieces. She watched his sullen face. It was as if he wanted to tear up their friendship with every rip.

'Everything's easy for you,' she cried. 'You don't know how lucky you are!'

'I don't know anything.' Joe tossed the scraps of paper across the floor. Cora felt suddenly suffocated by Joe's oppressive mood. Without another word she stormed out of the shop, slamming the door behind her, and ran down the street.

Carrie returns to the smart houses by the park. Silent as a cat, she climbs a fence and creeps through the communal gardens, scanning the houses until she spots a window left ajar, a window she might force open further. Fear floods through her, like fire in her blood. A heady mix of terror and excitement. She has come to relish the fear now, the thrill it gives her. Joe and his miserable moods and his accusations. He'll never feel this. He likes his safe, small world. Well, I'm not going to rot away in a cellar. While I've got breath in my body I'm going to live! She pushes open the window and climbs inside.

Wait.

Listen.

No sound but the drumming in her head, the pulse of being alive. Move as little as you can, take what's to hand. Silver salt and pepper pots stand on the nearest shelf. She takes them, rolls them up in a rag in her pocket to muffle the sound. That's all. Out she climbs without a knock or a creak … and away.

Carrie scrambles back through the gardens and over the fence and then she runs and runs, so fast that she feels she's flying and her breath is laughter, wild and triumphant and mad at the world. The night is hers, everything is hers. No one is going to make her stop feeling this. Not Joe, not anyone.

Carrie takes the salt and pepper pots to Skelly. 'You missed a trick, girl,' he says, spitting a gob of tobacco on the floor as he gives them a shine on his jacket sleeve. 'I bet there's a dainty little mustard pot feeling lonely now they're gone. They'd have fetched a better price together.' He sighs. 'Well, two's company, three's a crowd, eh?'

Carrie feels a fool. She'd remember to keep her nerve next time.

Skelly takes some coins from his purse, but as Carrie reaches out for them he closes his fist. 'You owe me something first.' She draws back her hand in alarm. His searching eyes glint in the candlelight. She edges towards the door.

'You have something of mine,' says Skelly, looking cruelly amused at her discomfort. 'You have my name, but you ain't traded fair.' Still, for a moment she doesn't understand.

'I don't do business with strangers. Not regular business,' he says.

It seems a fair trade for a thief's respect.

'Carrie,' she says, stretching out her hand once more.

'No more?'

Carrie shakes her head. 'There isn't any more.'

Skelly nods thoughtfully, then opens his fist and drops the coins into her hand.

She slips out into the dark alley, heart pounding, palms clammy with sweat. She has spoken her name. She feels stronger, a little more real.

With money in her pocket Carrie buys a bag of cockles and sits on the quay outside The Anchor, listening to the hearty talk and laughter around her. She watches the river, mesmerised by the ceaseless flow of water rushing to escape the city, destined to break on some exotic shore. A faint trace of spices drifts on the night air.

The serving boy sits down beside her.

'Shut your eyes,' he says. 'Go on, take a deep breath.' Carrie looks at him sharply, but he gives her an insistent nod. She closes her eyes.

'Smell that. That's the scent of Zanzibar Island come up from the big dock,' he says. 'Some nights you can smell all the spices of Africa round here …' Carrie's reverie is broken by a nudge in the arm. 'Most nights it's the stink of the sewers up from 'ammersmith!'

'Hey!' she cries, but the boy laughs, helps himself to a cockle, and saunters off.

Zanzibar. Carrie plays with the word in her head. Zanzibar. Could it really be possible to step onto a boat here and travel all the way to Africa? She imagines leaving the filthy, overcrowded city and crossing the ocean to a place where the sun always shines. As the sound of foreign voices murmurs in her ears Carrie's dream swells like a windblown sail and floats down the dirty river.

✧ 22 ✧

Cora sat outside the tavern in Farthing Court, watching a brood of rookery children squabble over a hoop. She wished she hadn't argued with Joe. She should have stayed and found a way to reassure him. He's afraid, that's why he lashed out at me, she thought. Afraid of losing his father's job, of having nowhere to live, afraid of crossing that counter to the other side. Cora knew she'd not been much of a friend to him recently. She was weary from lack of sleep, from the secrets she couldn't share. Those hateful secrets.

Cora noticed a tousle-haired girl in a dirty shift emerge from a house nearby, brandishing a wooden spoon. The girl strode over to the huddle of children, wielding her weapon above their heads and boldly snatched the hoop. At once a riot erupted, but she fought them all off and ran away, carrying the awkward hoop in her arms. The others raced after, shouting resentfully, all except one small girl, who sat down in the dirt and cried. Cora looked at the solitary, miserable f igure. Suddenly she realised how lonely she felt, imprisoned by her deception and lies. What would life be like without Joe's friendship? Those hours teaching him to read, playing with Pip, had been the happiest she'd ever spent. Maybe it wasn't too late to tell him everything. He already thought the worst of her anyway. Maybe it was worth the risk to make him understand. Cora got up and offered the little girl the crust of her bread. The girl stopped crying, wiped her tears away with a grubby sleeve and took the bread. She smiled shyly at Cora. If only it was always so easy to make things better, thought Cora. She'd go to see Joe straight away.

On her way to Mite Street Cora took a detour through the market to buy a barley sugar twist for Joe. As she put it in her pocket there was a loud crash of broken crockery. Cora looked up. On the opposite side of the road, between the boot barrow and the crockery stall, she saw a dark figure, framed in an archway. It was a girl in a black cloak, her head bowed, standing still as a statue while people passed back and forth along the street before her. Her face was hidden by a hood, but Cora could just make out a veil of chestnut hair that fell forward. As the girl reached up to tuck it back, the cloak fell away from her arm. There, underneath was the sleeve of a poppy red dress. A sleeve with a scalloped edge and tiny buttons – just like hers. That's not possible. Cora's mind started to swim. That cloak, that hair …

A pair of heavy horses pulled a dray stacked high with barrels through the crowd, obscuring her view. In the moment they took to pass, the girl disappeared. Cora ran across the road. She looked everywhere but there was no sign of her. Had she imagined it? No.

She turned to the butcher's boy beside her, cutting up meat on his block. Cora grabbed him by the arm. 'Did you see a girl just then, under that arch? A girl in a red dress, wearing a cloak?'

'Not likely. I was watching me cleaver.' The boy pulled his arm away and stuck up a bloody hand, displaying a scar where his little finger used to be. He laughed at Cora's shocked face.

'A girl with a red dress?' he said, going back to his work. 'I've seen her here before. She often hangs around.'

'Who is she?' Cora held her breath.

'Prob'ly a rookery girl, the way she eyes everything. Up to no good, like the rest of them,' said the boy, piling a heap of stewing meat onto a tray. 'I dunno her name.'

Cora walked away, feeling disturbed and confused. A strange thought occurred to her. *He didn't recognise me. He knows her but he didn't know me.* With a start she realised how Joe had been feeling, afraid of things not making sense. Cora reached up to tuck a loose lock of hair inside her hood and realised that the girl had done exactly the same, twisting the hair as she slid her fingers along its length and then flicking it over her shoulder. Carrie, in the red dress. In that red dress.

✒ 23 ✒

The more Cora tried to make sense of the girl she'd seen in the market, the more the boundary between what was real and imagined, between truth and pretence became blurred in her mind. It had to be a coincidence and yet she was certain it wasn't. She lost all her resolve to tell Joe the truth. It was almost as if this girl had deliberately appeared to stop her, to make her doubt herself.

Dusk fell, and Cora returned to the cellar without a word to anyone. She flung herself on her mattress, pulled her shawl over her head and tried to shut it all out. Still the girl haunted her darkness, standing so still, untouched by everyone who bustled around her. Cora knew she was waiting for her to speak her name. I won't say it, she vowed silently. I won't make it true. I won't say it. But deep down she knew it was already too late.

Several hours later Cora was woken by a noise. She propped herself up on her elbow and peered into the darkness. All was quiet outside. Nobody stirred in the cellar except the dog boy, who was tugging off his boots. She guessed that he'd woken her.

Cora lay back and shut her eyes again, but couldn't sleep. This was Carrie's hour. The time to put on her costume and play her part. Her costume. The red dress. Then Cora had an idea. Maybe the dress the girl had been wearing *had* been hers. Maybe she'd stolen it. That would explain everything.

Cora reached for her cloak and crept silently out of the cellar. On the other side of the yard the tavern light splashed across the cobbles, the energetic notes of a fiddle danced through the roar of a raucous song within. The chair mender sat smoking on his doorstep. Others trudged across the court on their weary way home. Cora slipped between the houses, moving quickly in the darkness. She fumbled with the lid of the barrel and reached inside.

Her fingers found the sack and felt the weight of the dress. She held it close, fingering the scalloped collar and the tiny pearl buttons, smelling the reek of tobacco smoke from The Anchor Inn. A voice in her head urged her to put it on. *Forget about what you think you saw. You need me. You made me. Let me live and I'll look after you.*

Cora stepped into the red dress and pulled it up over

her own. There is nothing to be afraid of, she told herself. Nothing except your own fear. This is real. I know it. I can touch it. She buttoned up the bodice and cuffs, swung the cloak around her shoulders and tugged the hood over her head.

Carrie crosses the court and enters the passage. A moment later she emerges on the street and walks out into the night. She is looking for something to make her forget.

She seeks out the wealthy crowd waiting for their carriages outside the opera house. She knows an escape route to a tunnel nearby where she can hide until it's safe to go home. Carrie positions herself behind the awning of a tobacco stall, watching the women fussing with their silks and furs as they discuss the performance, while the men attending them scan the street impatiently for a cab. She watches from the shadows for a glint of silver as the men pull handkerchiefs and cigarette cases from their pockets. Then she bows her head and moves close.

Ten minutes later she is crouching in the tunnel, laughing breathlessly as three fine cigar cases and a pocket watch chink together in her lap.

When Cora walked over to the tavern for her breakfast, she found Bess in a fluster.

'Oh, Cora! Everything's a shambles,' she cried. 'Ned the cook has gone and joined the army. He didn't give Father any word of warning and, to make matters worse, our Evie has gone with him! I'm left to roast the beef and pour the beer!'

'I'll help,' said Cora. 'What can I do?'

'Oh, you've saved my life! Here ...' She thrust a glass into Cora's hand and led her round behind the bar. 'I'll show you.'

Cora helped Bess all morning and enjoyed feeling useful. With much good-natured advice from the customers she soon mastered how to pour an acceptable pint of ale. My first honest work, she thought with pride. Most of the faces in the tavern were familiar and friendly, but one man praised the ale enthusiastically, saying he'd never been in there before.

'I usually drink at The Red Lion, that big coaching inn on Turnbull Street,' he told his neighbour at the bar. 'But there's no chance of a peaceful pint there this morning. Three coaches arrived all at once, two of them unexpected. The place is packed and everyone's running about in a panic. And to make matters worse, a woman with a voice like a foghorn is making a huge fuss and bother about a hatbox, stolen right there. You'd think someone had stolen her head. The barman said the stable boy thought a girl took it, a girl in a black cloak and a red dress.' He took a long draught of his ale. 'Hey, what's the matter, lass?'

Cora's face had turned white as a sheet. She swayed unsteadily. It couldn't be true. How could it be Carrie? She'd been here. Cora dropped the glass in her hand and rushed out of the door, leaving helpless Bess to clasp her head in despair.

Cora ran towards Turnbull Street, dodging carriages and wagons, almost knocking over a man selling paper windmills from a cart. When she got there she spotted the sign for The Red Lion. Pressing through the midday crowds she reached it and fell, breathless, against the wall of the coaching yard. She had to see for herself. She had to be sure. A carriage had just arrived. Stable boys were unbuckling the harness from a pair of steaming black horses, another boy swept up droppings while two coachmen, loaded with luggage, followed their passengers into the inn. Beside the door, which was hung with baskets of flowers, stood a life-size statue of a red lion. The whole scene buzzed with kitchen maids and potboys, market people and lunchtime drinkers. There'd be plenty of opportunity to slip in and take something left unattended, thought Cora. But she knew, without doubt, that she had never been there before. She stared at the street, afraid the cloaked figure might suddenly appear. It doesn't make sense. How can this girl be me?

She's not you, said a voice in her head. She's Carrie.

But Carrie is me. I created her. Even as she thought this, Cora began to doubt its truth. Hadn't that name haunted her ever since she could remember? From the moment she'd spoken it aloud, Carrie had had a hold over her. Now she seemed to have stepped out of Cora's story into the world. On the way back to Farthing Court, she stopped outside the gates of Walston Workhouse. Cora gripped the iron railings and stared through the bars. The yard was empty and silent, a peaceful sanctuary compared to the noisy clamour of the street. Cora swung round nervously to scan the sea of faces for a black hood, a flash of scarlet. She heard Martha's voice. *Go back where you came from.* Fletch whispered, *You ain't got the nerve!* Maybe she did belong in the house of the desperate and mad.

24

Cora walked quickly away from Walston. She turned a corner and then another, before finally allowing herself to slow down. Her hands shook and her mouth was dry. The draw of the workhouse was becoming harder to resist. And yet she knew there was no real sanctuary from what troubled her, except the truth. She felt the barley twist she'd bought for Joe still in her pocket. She would go and talk to him now. She had to make him understand. If she could be real and true with Joe she'd feel stronger, maybe everything would start making sense again.

Cora made her way to the pawnbroker's shop, constantly checking the crowds for a figure in black, a glimpse of red to prove that the girl had been a coincidence, just a stranger like herself, after all. When she reached the shop she was relieved to see that Joe was there alone.

'You've changed,' he said abruptly as she shut the door behind her.

Cora wasn't surprised any more by his odd, cold greeting. What she had to say wasn't going to be easy. 'I'm sorry I upset you the other day,' she began.

'You lied to me,' said Joe, without looking at her. 'You've been lying to me all along.' He turned away and started noisily re-arranging a set of hand-bells on a shelf.

'Joe, I've come to tell you everything.' Cora sat down on the trunk beside him.

'You don't need to tell me,' he said. 'I know. I know what you do.' At that moment a woman came into the shop with a bundle of clothes to pledge, followed by a couple of boys who'd been sent to redeem their father's ladder. Cora watched Joe attend to them, wondering what he meant. How could he have discovered she wasn't a teacher's assistant? Had he followed her to Farthing Court?

'No sign of Pa again,' said Joe when the new assistant returned from his break.

'You go for your lunch,' said the boy brightly. 'I'll be all right. You said it's quiet mid-week.' Joe nodded.

'I'll just go fetch my boots from the cobblers, then I'll eat out the back.' Joe fetched his jacket from its peg by the door. He ignored Cora, and walked out of the shop. She followed.

'I need to talk to you,' she said urgently, as she tried to

keep up with his march along the street. 'I promise I'll tell you the truth. Everything. No more secrets.'

Joe didn't reply at once, but a few steps down the road he stopped and looked her in the eye. 'I know it was you at The Red Lion this morning,' he said. Cora stared at him, astounded.

'A woman who came into the shop cleans at the pub. She told me what happened. The girl who stole the hatbox wore a black cloak and a red dress.'

'But that wasn't me! I wasn't there!' Cora grabbed her skirt. 'Look at this old rag, Joe, when have you ever seen me wear a red dress?'

'Ten minutes ago. Standing right outside the shop window.'

Cora looked at him, aghast. 'But you must have seen someone else,' she pleaded, unable to believe what she was hearing.

'I'm not stupid!' Joe frowned angrily. 'It was you, Carrie. Why are you doing this? I know your face. You looked straight at me with the hatbox in your arms. Why didn't you come in? Were you hoping Snub would be there alone, to take what you'd stolen?'

Cora gripped his sleeves. 'This is mad. It wasn't me. I'm telling you, you've got to believe me!'

'You've never told me the truth,' said Joe. 'How can I believe you? You're a liar, just like my father. Worse – you're a thief!' And with that he shrugged her off and hurried away into the crowd. Cora watched Joe disappear and her eyes welled with fierce, hot tears. That girl. That dress. Its vivid red burned in her mind. How could she put a stop to this? *I'll destroy it. If the dress is gone, Carrie can't exist any more.*

That night Cora waited until everyone in the cellar was asleep and Farthing Court was silent, then she went to the yard to fetch the dress. Five minutes walk down to the bridge and it would all be over. She imagined the red gown laying on the black river, floating away, rippling and folding until it was slowly drawn down below. Cora clutched it tight.

No.

She couldn't let it go. Once more she felt an overwhelming desire to put it on. Put it on and never take it off. The dress was part of her now. Her protection, her second skin. Wearing this she could walk away from that squalid cellar, from Joe and his accusations, and make something of herself. When she wore this red dress, it felt good to be alive.

In the nights that followed, Carrie sought out danger, dared herself with more audacious challenges, just to feel the thrill of the risk, the elation of emptying her pockets before Skelly's greedy eyes. And he nurtured the need, the hunger in her. She gave no thought to anything or anyone else.

In the mornings Cora woke in the dim, cold cellar, every day more tired and confused. She walked the streets, unable to settle her mind, watching for the mysterious figure that haunted her daylight hours. Cora often found herself wandering past the pawnshop in the hope that Joe might notice her and take pity, that he might beckon her in and somehow understand. She yearned for his company, his tall tales of eccentric customers, their mugs of hot chocolate in the store room as they read stories together, laughing at Pip tumbling somersaults in her lap. But the memory of those happy hours wore thin, like a dream too often recalled. Soon her nights seemed more real than her days.

25

A few days after the incident at the Red Lion, Cora returned to Farthing Court to find the invalid, Signor Peretti, now strong and well thanks to her care, sitting alone, whittling a stick. There was something strange about the scene and at first Cora couldn't think what was wrong. Then she realised. Nellie and her baby were gone.

'She wanted to say goodbye,' said Signor Peretti gently, seeing that Cora was upset. He brushed the shavings of wood from his lap. 'She didn't know where to look for you. Nobody knows where you go all day.'

Cora realised with a jolt that she'd been so completely absorbed in herself she hadn't brought anything for Nellie and the others for at least two days. 'Where did she go?'

'To the workhouse. Not half an hour ago. It was always her plan, you know.'

'Didn't anyone try to stop her?'

'Why?' said Signor Peretti. 'This is no place for a baby, growing up among rats and rubbish. They'll have a proper bed and regular meals at the workhouse, she said. And maybe she could work in the kitchen.'

'But I told her she didn't need to go to Walston,' cried Cora. 'I said I'd look after her.' If only she'd warned Nellie about the girls who'd disappeared. She had to stop them reaching the workhouse before it was too late. Cora set off as fast as she could, trying to guess the route Nellie might have taken, furious with herself for breaking her promise. But the closer she got to Walston the more her hope faded. When she finally reached the gate, the courtyard was empty, save for a washerwoman filling a pail from an outside tap and a starved-looking cat winding itself around her skirt. Cora couldn't bear to think the worst – that she was gone. She waited, scanning every access to the street, willing Nellie to appear. She had no idea how long she stood at the gate, but as dusk fell she knew her wait was in vain. Somewhere behind those dark, bleak windows, Nellie's baby would be crying for his mother. And who knew what Nellie's fate would be now. Would she disappear like the others, carried off in the dead of night by the Devil's coach?

With a heavy heart Cora turned away. She was lost in thought as she walked back towards Farthing Court, unaware that she'd wandered away from familiar streets. The clatter of running footsteps made her stop and look up. She was halfway along a narrow passage between derelict warehouse buildings. The only light came from candle glow in a high window ahead. The footsteps drew closer, louder, urgently tapping on the cobbles ahead. Cora waited, her heart beating fast. Even before a figure appeared at the end of the passage she knew who it would be. A billowing black cloak and a flash of scarlet. The girl was there. And then she was gone. The sound of her footsteps echoed away. Cora ran to the end of the passage, but the street before her was empty.

That night Cora dreamed she was chasing the girl in the red dress through a catacomb of candlelit cellars. Each room led to another, strewn with rubbish, infested with rats. At last, breathless and tired, Cora caught up. The girl had brought her to a cavernous chamber, unlike the others, and stopped before a vast, heavy door, framed by an iron arch.

'Don't open it,' cried Cora. 'You mustn't go in there!' But as the girl touched the door it swung open. Beyond it was a black carriage with a pair of black horses, but no coachman. The girl in the red dress pulled down the step and climbed inside.

'Don't go!' cried Cora. She tried to reach out but was unable to move. The girl sat at the window and drew back her hood. It was Nellie, solemn and pale. The wheels began to roll and Cora stared in horror at their livery: painted red serpents swallowing their tails. The Devil's coach.

❧ 26 ❧

Carrie has brought a pair of fine kid gloves to Skelly. A precious prize, snatched from the foyer of the opera house itself. She watches him examine them in the candlelight, remembering with pleasure the performance she gave to get them.

Skelly kneads the soft leather between his finger and thumb thoughtfully. He hesitates. Something's not right. But he smiles. 'How would you like to earn some real money? A bright girl like you could do better.'

Carrie is intrigued. Skelly leans close and she has to mask her revulsion at his foul breath with her hand.

'Information, that's my real business,' he murmurs. 'And something's come to my attention that might make us both a tidy sum. Pigment.'

Pigment? Carrie doesn't understand.

'Paint pigment – valuable stuff to them artists at the Academy. A rare consignment is going to be stored at a certain warehouse near here. Even a few ounces would fetch a pretty price.' He eyes her keenly. 'Interested?'

Carrie nods, waiting to hear what she'll have to do. 'It's simple enough,' says Skelly. 'Someone small conceals themselves inside the warehouse, earlier in the day, and watches to see where the pigment's stored. Then, in the dead of night, under cover of darkness, they just walk out with the package in their arms.'

'It'll be locked at night,' says Carrie. 'Somebody would have to be very small to slip under the door.'

Skelly smiles. 'You'd have to trust me, Carrie, my dear. A snip of the chain from outside and it's open sesame.'

'Then you could walk in and take it yourself.'

Skelly takes a long draught of his ale. 'They're as big as cathedral vaults, those warehouses. I'd be searching all night. But if you saw where they stored the packages when they came in, well, it's straight to it and out. Job done.'

Carrie doesn't like the idea of being locked in the warehouse at night, but she does like the challenge – and the promise of a handsome price.

Next day she walks right in and delivers a letter to the foreman.

'No, you've got the wrong man,' he says. 'There isn't a Mr Montague here. I'm Marshall. Try Porter's, down the road.'

'What do you keep in all those packages?' Carrie says, idly casting her eye over a stack of bales close to the foreman's office, bales large enough to conceal somebody who wanted to hide.

'Oh, we have everything come in here,' says the foreman. 'Coffee, sugar, even ostrich feathers and turtle shells.'

Carrie smiles. 'It's like a treasure house.'

Cora walked along a wide, tree-lined avenue in the park. Gazing up at the bare branches, she could almost believe she was back in the country. She remembered the oak tree she used to climb to hide from Martha. Life had been so much simpler then. And no matter how miserable she felt, she could always curl up in a comfortable bed at night. *I never knew how lucky I was.*

'Paa-per, paa-per! Lunnon Gazette!'

The newsboy's cry reminded Cora where she was. Dry leaves rattled at her feet. Autumn was turning to winter, to dark days and long nights. She found an empty bench and sat down, pulling her shawl over her head with a shiver. A lace handkerchief tumbled past her in the breeze. Was it too late now for that white dress in the sunny room she'd dreamed of? How could she pursue something wholesome, something good, when lies and secrets had become her currency?

As dusk started to fall, a mist rose from the river. The damp penetrated her thin clothes. She got up to make her way back to the rookery. The winding path through the park entered a thicket of shrubs. Here, the light was dim and the mist dense as fog.

Cora didn't hear a sound until the girl appeared before her. She stopped, frozen to the spot. The girl stood still with her head lowered, her face obscured by the hood, only a few feet away. Close enough for Cora to recognise the cloak, the cuffs of that red dress.

'Who ... who are you?' she stuttered. 'Why do you follow me?'

The girl raised her head and pulled back the hood. Cora stared in disbelief. Locks of chestnut hair tumbled forward, around her own, solemn face. Cora's mind reeled, her legs felt weak. It was impossible.

'I don't understand!' she gasped. 'Tell me ...'

The girl slowly shook her head. Cora felt faint and giddy. She knew this girl, she knew that sorrow in her eyes. She took a step forward and reached out her hand, but, as if they were engaged in a dreamlike dance, the girl stepped backwards and at once the conspiring mist swallowed her up. Cora darted forwards but the girl had vanished, like a vision, like a spectre. Like a ghost.

❦ 27 ❧

Cora sat on the pavement outside the pawnbroker's shop early next morning, clutching her bag. She hadn't slept all night but it didn't matter. Nothing mattered any more, except her determination to talk to Joe. All her exhausted will was fixed upon it. He had to be there, he had to listen to her this time and help her open her mother's box.

Through the long night, her mind had struggled to make sense of everything. What was real? What was her own invention? When she started to think she was going mad, one thing had anchored her to reality – her mother's box. It was the only testament to who she really was. Now she had to look inside. She was convinced that she'd find herself there. Her true self, before ghosts and stories, before lies and secrets, before even Elijah had given her his name. Cora knew Joe's father had boxes of old keys in the store room. One of them had to fit. If not, she was going to ask Joe to break the box open. She was sure he'd be able to do it. Why hadn't she thought of it before? Whatever was inside, she wanted him to see it too. Maybe then he would finally trust her. But everything now depended on whether he would even see her at all.

When Joe came to the door to open up the shop he was astonished to find Cora on the step, looking grey and gaunt. Still angry and yet suddenly afraid for her, his heart fought with his head. Before he could decide what to do, Pip came bounding out of the shop. With excited squeaking he clambered over Cora's bag and onto her lap. Pip took her face in his tiny hands and kissed it all over. Cora smiled.

'Come on in,' said Joe reluctantly. 'Pa just made a pot of tea.'

Cora followed Joe upstairs to the parlour, where they found Mr Tally adjusting his collar in the mirror.

'Look who I found, Pa,' said Joe. 'Is there any more tea in the pot?'

'You look after her, son,' said Mr Tally with a concerned frown. 'I've got to go and get ready for business downstairs.'

'What's happened to you, then?' said Joe, as Pip rocked quietly in Cora's lap.

'I've got so much to tell you, Joe,' she said. 'I'm so sorry

I lied that very first day we met. I know I can't expect you to believe anything else I say, but I promise I'll only tell you the truth from now on.'

'I want to believe you,' Joe said, 'but I'm not stupid. You treated me like a fool. I only wanted you to tell me the truth.'

Cora looked him straight in the eye and took a deep breath. 'First you must believe that I wasn't the girl in the red dress that you saw that morning, outside the shop. I promise you, no matter how much she looked like me, I was somewhere else that morning and one day I'll be able to prove it to you.'

Joe could see how earnest she was. Still, he wasn't convinced. He trusted his own eyes.

Cora opened her bag and pulled out the painted box.

'This belonged to my mother,' she said. 'She died when I was very young. It's all I have that belonged to her.'

'Have you really just come here to pawn an old box?'

'Oh, no!' Cora shook it and the box rustled and rattled. 'When I was little I used to talk to it and tell myself the sound it made was my mother's voice answering, all muffled and squashed inside.' She laughed bitterly, and Joe was surprised at how different she sounded, how desperate. She put the box into his hands. 'Now I need her to talk to me, Joe. It doesn't have a key and I need to open it. It's the only way I can find the truth for myself and explain to you who I really am. Will you help me?'

Joe was curious. He examined the box and shook it for himself. 'Why haven't you ever opened it before?'

'It's so precious I never wanted to break it open. But I have to know what's inside now, no matter what.'

Joe looked at her pleading face. I suppose there is a chance I was wrong, he thought. If whatever was inside the box would clear things up somehow, it was worth a try. 'Well, we've got loads of keys downstairs in the storeroom,' he said. 'Come on, let's have a go.'

Cora was already on her feet, heading for the door.

Joe heaved two heavy boxes of keys off a low shelf and fetched a third from a cupboard. Cora set to work, delving among the keys to find one that might fit, while Joe went upstairs to warm up some soup left over from supper the night before. He returned with a bowl of hot soup and a plate of bread and cheese and Cora ate everything gratefully. Joe was pleased to see her look better for it. He realised how much he'd missed her.

Before long mounds of discarded keys piled up around them.

'If we can't find one that fits I could try unscrewing the hinges of the box,' suggested Joe, but Cora was determined to try every one first. At last her persistence was rewarded. She found a brass key that slipped easily into the lock and turned with a click. Cora took a deep breath. It was difficult to believe that she was about to find out what had been hidden for so long.

She lifted the lid.

The box contained three small parcels, wrapped in brown paper with a label tied to each. Cora picked one up and turned over the label to read it. Joe saw her face turn pale. Instead of opening the package she just stared. He looked at the words written on the label. *For Carrie.*

Cora couldn't speak. The sight of that name shook her to the bone. How could Carrie be here, in her mother's box? These presents couldn't have been for anyone else but her. She'd been hoping for a simple truth, an identity she could believe in, but now ... nothing made sense.

'Don't you want to open the presents?' asked Joe. 'I thought you wanted to know what was inside?'

Cora nodded silently. Slowly, with trembling hands, she untied the parcel in her lap. Inside lay a carved wooden horse with a string mane and tail. Joe handed her the second parcel, which contained a child's necklace made of painted beads. The third had a familiar feel. Cora made a tear in the paper and two dark eyes gazed out. A head of plaited hair and a dress made from a scrap of blue gingham. It was Belle's twin, clean and new. A tiny rag doll for a child named Carrie.

Joe waited for Cora to say something, to tell him the truth, like she'd promised, but she just looked at the gifts in bewilderment. A hint of long forgotten memory stirred somewhere deep in her mind, but it was overshadowed by the sight of that name. Carrie. *You've taken over my life. Now, you've stolen my past.*

For the first time, Carrie is in no mood to seek excitement. She walks down to The Anchor Inn and sits on the wall at the wharfside, watching flecks of lamplight shimmy on the water.

'You drinking?' says the potboy as he rattles past with a tray of tankards. She shakes her head. Suddenly a boot swings out beside her and kicks a discarded oyster shell onto the muddy bank.

'I wasn't expecting to see your face round here,' says Skelly, sitting himself on an upturned tub.

With a shock Carrie realises it is the night she is supposed to be hidden in the warehouse. 'I was coming to tell you,' she says, trying not to sound flustered. 'Something happened ...'

Skelly peers at her with narrow eyes. 'You wouldn't be taking me for a fool, Miss Carrie?' His words slide out like a drawn blade. She senses something is wrong. Slowly he holds out his hand. 'If you've been bold enough to come back here you must have something for me?'

'I don't understand,' she says.

'You were seen last night running from the warehouse. Drake the barman caught sight of you on his way home late. It was that blood red dress he couldn't mistake.' In a flash he grips her by both wrists and pulls her to her feet.

'You're hurting, let me go.'

'We don't double cross our friends, do we?' He smiles cruelly at her pain.

Carrie knows it would be useless to deny she was at the warehouse, yet she can't tell him the truth. She doesn't know what the truth is. 'I wouldn't cheat you,' she says, keeping her voice steady. 'I'll fetch the package. I left it hidden safely last night. I only stopped here to meet a friend. I'll go back for it now.'

Skelly releases his grip and lets her go, but he still eyes her suspiciously. He has never had reason not to trust her before, but there is something odd about the whole business. As he watches her hurry away he fingers a length of cord in his pocket. She'll regret it if she crosses him.

28

When Mr Tally finished work that evening and tramped wearily upstairs to the parlour, he found Joe sitting at the table, fingering the navy medal.

'How many people have a medal like this, do you think, Pa?' Joe asked.

'Oh, I don't know, son,' said Mr Tally, sitting down to untie his boots. 'They probably give them out to lots of men.' He reached for his slippers.

'I know somebody who got one, just the same as you.' He turned the medal over and read out the name. 'Patrick O'Leary.'

Mr Tally dropped his slippers. The colour drained from his face.

'Carrie's been teaching me to read,' said Joe, studying his father's face intently. 'I wanted to keep it a surprise.'

'Well, it certainly is.'

'Why did you lie to me, Pa?' cried Joe, tossing the medal into his father's hand. 'This isn't yours at all, is it? I've always believed you. I've always believed everything you told me!'

Mr Tally pulled his handkerchief from his pocket and wiped his brow.

'Ah, Joe!' he sighed. 'I've been such a fool.' He shook his head sorrowfully. 'I've been telling you stories. That's all they've been.'

So, it was true. Joe had been hoping with all his heart that there was some simple explanation, however strange. Anything but this.

'Why, Pa? What was wrong with the truth?'

'The truth was ugly, lad. I didn't want to put ugly things in your head.'

Joe looked at his father, his hero – a man he'd always believed would never lie. Suddenly he didn't want to know, he just wanted things to go back to how they'd always been.

'When you were a baby I went to prison, Joe.' Mr Tally hung his head in shame.

Joe couldn't believe his ears. 'But what did you do, Pa?'

'I went because of what I didn't do,' said Mr Tally. 'I kept quiet to protect a friend who'd done something bad, Joe, when I should have spoken out against him. I was a young man then, without courage.'

Joe tried to take it in. His pa wasn't a hero at all, but a coward and a liar? He felt angry, and yet afraid. With those few words his father was destroying everything he'd believed in, everything that was right and good. Joe looked up, not knowing what to say and was shocked by the pain he saw on his father's face, making him suddenly look years older. Joe's anger passed. He saw at once that the confession had hurt his pa even more than it had hurt him. What a lonely secret to have carried for so long.

'I was away from you and your mother for three years,' his father said sadly. 'I asked her to tell you I'd gone to sea, because I was ashamed. When I came out, your mother died a month later and I didn't want to make things worse, I just kept up the pretence. There never seemed a good moment to tell you the truth. Later on there were so many times I nearly told you, but I was afraid you'd think ill of me, son. I dreaded that.'

'Oh, Pa!' Joe flung his arms around his father and hugged him tight. 'I could never think ill of you. Whatever you did, you did it for your friend and for me. That's better than being a book hero.' He felt a huge sense of relief.

Mr Tally sighed deeply. 'You're a good boy, Joe. Your mother would be proud of you.'

For a moment they sat in silence, each privately vowing never to be afraid to speak of difficult things again. That goes for Carrie, too, thought Joe. She'd said she was going to tell him the truth that morning, but she'd left without telling him anything at all. He would make her tell him next time.

'But what about the medal and the shipwreck and Captain Bristow?' Joe asked his father.

'The medal was brought in to the shop one day. I never expected you to read the name on it. The rest was a story from a book that Old Mr Snub read to me years ago. I told it to you once, Joe, and you asked for it over again. As time went by I added to it, of course, just to see your eyes sparkle. But once I'd started, how could I tell you the truth?'

Mr Tally got up and took a book from his desk drawer. 'I don't know why I kept this, but it seems you can read it for yourself now.'

Joe took the book from his father's hands. 'It's still a good story, even though it's not true,' he said.

Mr Tally smiled.

'Will you tell me something else, Pa? said Joe slowly. 'Where do you go, when you go out so often?'

His father looked surprised for a moment, then a distant, tender look came into his eye, a look Joe had never seen before. 'Well, son,' he said gently, 'maybe it's time there was something to tell there, but that's one secret that will have to wait until tomorrow.' He stood up, looking suddenly brighter and younger, Joe thought, as if he'd shed all his worries with his mysterious words. And nothing Joe said would make Mr Tally explain himself further on the subject.

Later, as they sat over their supper Joe had one last question. 'Was it right, Pa, sticking up for a friend when they did something bad?'

'I had lots of time to think about that,' said his father, folding the napkin in his lap.

'What did you decide?'

'That a real friend wouldn't put you in that position, Joe.'

Carrie hurries away from the wharf knowing that the girl in the red dress, whoever, whatever she is, has ruined her business with Skelly. It is over. The dark streets taunt her with shifting shadows and flashes of colour in the night. By the time she reaches the entrance to Farthing Court her nerves are shaken. Carrie stands by the barrel in the dark yard and unbuttons the red dress. As she reaches the last button she stops. Cora has no future of her own, that white dress in a sunny room will always be just a dream. The red dress is real. She can touch it. It was Carrie's name in the box. Why be Cora any longer?

Carrie buttons up the dress again. It is time to decide her own fate. A low voice sings in her head, the voice of blind Nelson, the sailor. 'Oh, for a soft and gentle wind, I heard a fair one cry, but give to me the roaring breeze and the white waves heaving high.' She will take a boat down the river and across the sea. A boat to Zanzibar Island.

Carrie spends the night in the church vestry. Early in the morning she sets out to walk the streets. She needs to find something valuable to pay her passage. She makes her way to a row of grand houses beside the river. Now she hides there under a bush, concealed by the creeping river mist. She watches the households wake; shutters are opened, servants come and go, lighting fires and laying breakfast tables. Cutlery glints and glass sparkles. Carrie creeps nearer, crouching behind a stone urn. She gazes through a window at a pair of ornate silver candlesticks on the mantelpiece. Here is her ticket.

❦ 29 ❦

When Joe opened up the shop that morning to let the new man in, his father appeared beside him, dressed in his coat and hat.

'Where are you going, Pa?' said Joe. 'It's Snub's day off, you can't leave us alone!'

'Oh, you two can manage well enough for a while,' said Mr Tally, an unusual brightness to his voice. 'Get Pip to help. I won't be long this time, I hope. Wish me luck!' And with that he gave them both a smile and went off briskly down the street.

Joe's heart sank. Hadn't he promised there'd be no more secrets? He picked up the broom and began to sweep the floor angrily. He'd really believed things would be better now. Perhaps nothing had really changed after all.

An hour later, Joe's father returned with a woman at his side.

'This is Rose,' said Mr Tally. His face beamed with pride.

Joe watched as his father fussed about, finding Rose a chair and relieving her of her umbrella and gloves. There was a warmth and an ease about this kind-faced woman. But who was she?

'Won't you say anything, Joe?' said Mr Tally, the light in his eyes fading at the sight of Joe's bewilderment.

'You've given him a shock, Tom.' Rose squeezed his father's arm gently. 'I'm Mr Snub's aunt, Joe,' she said.

'Oh, I see,' said Joe, although he didn't. This smiling, friendly woman couldn't be less like Snub. Had she come to throw them out?

'Well,' exclaimed Rose. 'Shall we all have a cup of tea? Joe and I can make it if he shows me where everything is.'

As if in a dream, Joe found himself following a fur-trimmed coat and the scent of perfume upstairs to the parlour.

The tea didn't appear for some time. Rose had plenty to tell Joe first. 'It's on my account that your father has been so secretive these last few months, Joe,' she said. 'I'm sorry.' She told him how Mr Tally had come to her house one day to deliver a letter when Snub was ill and how a friendship had grown between them.

'It could have made things very awkward with Mr Snub if word got out. I own the shop, Joe, you see, and Mr Snub's been pestering me lately about inheriting. But now I've got to know your father better, well, grown very fond, we have …' Rose winked. 'I'm no business woman, Joe, but I do know human nature and I don't like a man who thinks only of his purse and profit. Let's just say that things are not going to turn out the way Mr Snub expects.'

Rose got up and took off her coat, leaving Joe to consider the meaning of her words. He thought he understood. His father and Rose grown fond? The shop not going to Snub? It was too much to take in at once.

'Now, where do we keep the tea?' said Rose, inspecting the cupboards. 'I'd better know where everything is.'

So this was Pa's secret! Suddenly Joe could hardly contain his smile.

Rose stayed at the shop all day and even took a turn behind the counter, parcelling up the pledges.

At midday Mr Tally went out to fetch lunch for them all. While he was gone, Joe showed Rose around the store rooms. When they came to the old chaise longue Rose paused and picked up the painted box Cora had left lying on the cushion in her sudden hurry to leave.

To Joe's surprise she seemed intrigued and sat down to examine it. 'I've seen this box before, a long time ago,' she said wistfully, gazing at the parcels inside.

'Where?'

'At Walston Workhouse. I used to do charitable work there, visiting the women who were sick.'

'Who did it belong to?' asked Joe. Could it be that Rose might tell him something of Carrie's mysterious past?

'I can't recall the woman's name. She was young, but gravely ill with consumption when I met her.' Rose grew sad. 'This box was all she owned in the world. I remember it because she kept telling me there was a bad secret inside.'

Joe looked at the carved horse, the bead necklace and the little rag doll. How could there be anything sinister about those toys?

'I sat and comforted her all night,' said Rose. 'She was weak but she wanted to tell me her story. Many of them wanted to talk when they felt the end was near, to put themselves at ease. It seemed that her husband had died soon after they were married and then a few weeks later she discovered she was expecting a baby. With no one to support her, she wrote to his parents, asking them to send money. When her time came she gave birth to twins, two little girls, but only one survived. She was alone and afraid. She couldn't pay the rent or work, so she told a lie that haunted her for the rest of her life. She sent word that she had two daughters, asking them to send her more.'

'So the lie was her secret?' said Joe, feeling sorry for Carrie and her mother. No wonder she didn't want to talk about her past.

'Yes,' said Rose. 'The poor woman kept crying for both her babies, as if she really believed she still had two. The strain had muddled her mind. She'd given the baby a name. For her, it lived. These things in the box must have reminded her of what she'd done. I think she kept them as a punishment.'

'Did the grandparents send money?' asked Joe.

'Apparently they sent a little, and these presents for the children,' said Rose, 'but it wasn't enough. She couldn't pay her rent and became homeless, and then she fell ill and had nowhere to go but the workhouse.'

'What happened to the baby?' asked Joe.

'She was taken away soon after they arrived.'

Joe had heard enough gossip about conditions in Walston Workhouse to imagine life there must have been harsh for a child.

'The woman died early in the morning,' said Rose. 'I gave the box to the matron and told her it belonged to the child, but I've no idea if it ever reached her.'

Joe knew that Carrie had received the box, but he couldn't understand why she'd seemed so shocked by what she'd found inside. Would she feel happier if he told her Rose's story? Would he even get the chance? She'd left in such a state of distress he wondered whether he'd ever see her again.

Rose and Joe were roused from their melancholy thoughts by the arrival of Mr Tally, brimming with enthusiasm for his fine oysters, his marvellous apple pie and what a wonderful day to be alive!

The afternoon was very merry. Mr Tally sent the new man home and shut the shop early, then Rose insisted that she treat them all to an evening at the Music Hall.

Only Pip was at home that evening when a tiny scratching sound disturbed the silence downstairs. A click. And then the handle of the back door turned silently. A cloaked figure slipped inside. It closed the door, paused to listen a moment, then moved quickly towards the staircase. The first step creaked underfoot. Pip scrambled onto Joe's bed and buried himself under the bedclothes.

Ɂ 30 Ɂ

arrie drops her sack gently over the gate and climbs after it into the garden beyond. She creeps through the shrubbery, across the lawn and up to the house. There she crouches beneath a tiny window with a broken latch. Moonlight slips between the half-drawn curtains, glistening on a pair of silver candlesticks on the mantelpiece within.

Carrie takes Pip out of the sack and strokes his puzzled head.

'Look, Pip – pretty things! Bring them to me. Lovely shiny silver.' She lifts him up to the tiny window and pushes it open.

Pip quizzes her a moment, then his beady eyes catch sight of the candlesticks. He pulls himself up and drops down inside the room. Carrie holds her breath. The candlesticks aren't the only objects that attract Pip. He scampers among the tables, picking up anything that sparkles. Carrie watches, her fists clenched, muttering instructions under her breath.

At last Pip swings round, almost knocking over an inkpot, and heads for the mantelpiece. The candlestick is weighty, but Pip is used to heavy parcels at the shop. Carefully he carries it across the room and lifts it up to the window. Carrie takes it from him.

'Good boy, Pip. Get the other one,' she hisses. 'Bring it to me!' She points and Pip bounds back to the mantelpiece.

This time when Pip returns to the window he won't let the candlestick go. Carrie reaches in, trying to pull it out of his hands, but Pip seems determined to carry it himself, as if he thinks one candlestick each is a fair reward for his strange night's work.

Something distracts him. Carrie looks up. The girl in the red dress steps into the doorway of the room, her face pale as marble. It's impossible. You can haunt Cora but not me! Pip looks back and forth at the two girls, confused.

'Pip! Come away!' But as Carrie calls out he drops the candlestick. It clatters to the floor. The girl vanishes. A moment later light glows in the hall beyond. Pip squeaks in alarm and flings himself up to the window, reaching for Carrie, who grabs his hand. Hurried footsteps approach. Pip twists round to see who is coming and suddenly cries out with pain. He falls from her grasp and lies motionless on the floor.

Carrie grabs the other candlestick and runs. She flees through the garden, flings herself over the gate and runs down the street towards the river. What has she done? She reaches a bridge and stops to catch her breath. Carrie is gripped by Cora's fear. The mask falls away; it can no longer protect her. Joe will never, never forgive her. She stares into the water. The deep, dark, river fills her eyes and her mind, escaping away beneath her. Escape! She throws off the cloak and starts to take off the dress.

It's my life! Mine. She's ripping the buttons now, hearing hurried footsteps approach the bridge. If she can get rid of this hateful dress she'll be free. She pulls her arms out of the sleeves and tears at the waist, ripping it off her body, stepping out of the skirt. The footsteps are coming closer, faster, but she daren't look back. She bundles the cloak and dress together.

She hears the splash of the bundle hitting the water below, and a man grabs her from behind. 'You're coming with me.'

◇◇ 31 ◇◇

ora spent the night in a police cell, shivering on a hard bench without a blanket. She couldn't recall how she'd got there. All she remembered was the relief of that sound, a heavy slap as the bundle of clothes hit the water. The dress was gone, the lies and pretence. Carrie was gone forever. What was left felt small and cold and afraid. But however miserable, it was real at last.

Now, all she could think about was the sight of Pip's twisted body sprawled on the floor of the house and how frantic Joe would be when he discovered Pip was missing. How could she ever tell him what she'd done? Cora wished she'd jumped into that river herself.

Her only comfort was a grimy lantern that had been left

on a table in the room outside her cell. The only sound, a monotonous patter of rainfall. She gazed at a small window, high up the wall, which looked out at street level onto the pavement outside. There she counted six bars, as brutal as the barred windows at the workhouse, locking her away. What brought me to this? When was my fate cast? Was it the day Fletch found me? The day Elijah died? Or even the day I was born? She curled up on the bench, shut her eyes and tried to escape into sleep.

But sleep tormented her again with the memory of Pip's tiny face at the window as he tried to climb out of the house, clattering the candlestick against the windowpane. Clattering, tapping against the glass.

Tap, tap, tap.

The noise woke her. Cora blinked wearily and yawned. The room had grown dim. Something close to the door of her cell was masking the light. She sat up and rubbed her eyes. Standing before her was the girl in the red dress. She'd thought it was over.

'Who are you?' Her eyes grew sharper in the gloom. The girl stood in silence, with her back to the lantern, casting a shadow between them. Slowly Cora got up and came close. The girl stepped aside and pushed her hood away so that the light slanted across her face. It was like looking in a mirror. My face, my eyes, thought Cora, but I don't know you.

'Who are you?' she whispered again. 'Am I dreaming?'

'No.' The voice was her own but sounded strange coming from another.

'Then you are a ghost?'

'No.' Cora remembered the footsteps she'd heard in the passage, the stolen hatbox. This girl was alive, her green eyes bright, her pale cheeks pink from the cold. But she was impossible. Cora reached nervously through the bars, her fingers touched the dress she knew so well and her heart missed a beat.

'I have come to say farewell.'

'I don't understand. Where did you come from? Why have you been haunting me?'

'You made me, Cora. You willed me into being.'

'How?'

'When you call something by its name you bring it to life. You allow it to live in your mind.'

'But Carrie was …'

'A way to hide from your guilt.'

'I had no choice.'

The girl said nothing.

'All those things you did …'

'Brought you here, to face your conscience.'

They stared at each other. Cora looked long and hard into the girl's eyes, into her own eyes. Deep into her own heart.

'Are you real, or in my mind?' she whispered.

'I'm as real as you need me to be.'

Cora grasped the bars of the cell. 'What will happen to me?'

'Believe in yourself, Cora.' The girl took a step away. 'Believe and your story will begin.'

'Wait! Don't go.' Cora pushed her hand between the bars but the girl pulled the hood over her head and swung away. The lantern went out and Cora was left in the dark. She crumpled onto the bench with her head in her hands, drained and bewildered. She had never felt so utterly alone. But slowly, as she sat there, Cora began to feel strangely calm. She breathed easy and with each breath her fear and confusion melted away. Had the girl been real? It didn't matter any more. Her mind cleared and she knew she had found a kind of truth at last. It was within herself.

Cora watched first light glisten on the rain-washed cobbles. Sparrows sang in the street. A fresh, new day began. The bright sparkling reminded her of a sunny room, a white dress laid upon a plump feather bed. Another window, open wide.

∾ 32 ∾

Joe stood at the window of the pawnbroker's shop, watching the world outside for the sight of a tiny monkey in a blue waistcoat. He was sure that whoever picked the lock on the store-room door the night before must have come deliberately to steal Pip. They hadn't taken a single thing from the shop.

'He'll be back, son. Don't worry.' Mr Tally brought him a cup of hot chocolate. 'I'm sure the burglar came for the silver, not for Pip. He must have made a noise, which frightened the intruder away, and then escaped himself. Pip's probably having a great adventure somewhere, but he'll be back for his dinner, you'll see.' Joe wanted to believe him. Everything should have been happy that morning, now that his father was his old self again and Rose was to be part of their lives.

'Good riddance,' said Snub. 'I'll be passing the pastry man this afternoon on my way to visit my aunt about business – I shall ask whether he is serving monkey pie today!'

Joe was furious. For a moment he wondered if Snub himself had taken Pip away.

'Snub!' said Mr Tally sharply, sensing the dangerous tension between them. 'Will you help me move some boxes in the attic?' Snub couldn't help a triumphant sneer in Joe's direction as he followed Mr Tally up the stairs. But Joe consoled himself with the knowledge that Mr Snub had a surprise waiting for him when he went to visit his aunt.

Five minutes later, a lady with a basket opened the door of the shop. As the bell hanging on the door rang out, her basket started to wobble bizarrely as if it had a life of its own. Joe watched her struggle to carry it to the counter, shaking her bonnet loose in the process. As soon as she put it down, out of the cover shot a tiny hand, followed by an excited, furry face.

'Pip!' Joe scooped him up in his arms. 'Where did you find him? Is he all right?' Pip clung tight to Joe's neck, chattering excitedly.

'He's just had a bump,' said the woman, fixing her bonnet back with a pin. 'Somebody put him through the window of my master's house. Lucky for you I recognised him.'

'Pip!' exclaimed Joe. 'Were you cleaning windows?'

'Stealing candlesticks, he was,' said the woman, wagging a finger at Pip. 'Or he would have done if the burglar had got away with it.'

'What burglar?' asked Joe. 'Somebody broke in and took him last night. I never thought I'd see him again.'

'It was my husband who saw her. A girl in a black cloak and a red dress. The police arrested her.'

Joe was shocked. Could it really have been Carrie? He played out the scene. It would have been easy for her to tempt Pip away. How could she use him to steal and leave him injured in a stranger's house? Joe felt betrayed. *She came to me, promising to tell the truth and I helped her. I believed her.*

'I know that girl,' he said. 'She used to be my friend.'

'I'm afraid she's a burglar too,' said Mrs Bagwell. 'My husband said he'd heard about her before, a girl just like that in a red dress. She stole a pair of boots from our cobbler once and gave him the slip.'

'At least you're safe, Pip, and come to no harm,' Joe thanked the woman, wishing he had something to give her, but she knew his situation and accepted his thanks with an understanding smile. She shook Pip's tiny hand with affection. 'I don't think the officer from Salt Lane police station will need to take your statement! Now I must be off home to polish your little fingerprints off that candlestick.'

So it was true. Joe sighed as he cut up an apple for Pip. No wonder Carrie had never told him the truth. What would he have done if he'd known? After all, they'd sold her things in the shop. Suppose stolen goods had been traced back to his father? He'd have gone to prison, or worse. Had she lied to protect us, he wondered, just like Pa tried to protect his friend? Joe thought about what he really knew, what he could be sure of – all the hours they'd spent together, laughing over his clumsy letters, playing with Pip. No matter what else Carrie had done, he knew her as a friend, not a thief. Why hadn't she trusted him? Joe remembered the story of the box. He couldn't guess what sort of life she'd had since she'd left the workhouse, what had led her to this. Was it too late to help now?

❦ 33 ❦

Church bells struck eight as a carriage drew up outside the police station that morning. Cora sat absently watching the passing multitude of legs, skirts, dogs, cats, and pram wheels as she thought over the night before. There was no reason to lie any more. Carrie was gone. She would tell the truth and face the consequences of what she'd done. It's what Elijah had taught her so long ago. How could she have forgotten?

As the passers-by dispersed briefly, Cora noticed one of the carriage wheels drawn up beside the pavement. A red snake around the black hub. She remembered the words of the old woman outside the workhouse. The Devil's coach with red serpents riding the wheels! Could this be the coach that took girls from Walston? What was it doing here? Cora climbed up onto the bench and strained to see better but her view was obscured by the crowd once more. A door slammed above and voices and footsteps approached, coming down the basement stairs. Cora was suddenly filled with dread. Was it here for her?

A policeman entered the room, followed by a tall, white-haired man in a long black coat, embroidered waistcoat and top hat. He carried a silver-tipped cane. Cora clambered off the bench and retreated to the back of the cell.

'You can leave us, Sergeant Horner,' said the man. The policeman made a polite bow and withdrew.

The man looked at Cora for an uncomfortably long time before he spoke. 'Do you know who I am?' he said at last.

'No, Sir,' said Cora nervously. She looked at the cane and remembered the day Martha's brother had arrived at the cottage. This time she would escape before she let anyone take her away. She'd run for it as soon as they opened the door.

'It was my house that you and your nimble friend the monkey broke into last night.'

'Pip!' Cora gasped.

'I shouldn't think the monkey suffered anything more than indigestion after a very large breakfast this morning,' said the man. 'He was fussed over by my housekeeper and then taken back to where he belongs.'

Cora almost cried with relief. Pip alive and reunited with Joe! But what now? What did this man want with her?

He asked her name. She remembered her vow not to lie any more. 'Cora, Sir,' she said, 'Cora Parry.' It seemed a long time since she'd spoken Elijah's name. It felt like an old friend from another life. She held her head a little higher.

'Do you have family? Where is your home?'

'No, Sir,' she answered. 'No family and nowhere to go.'

The man looked about for a chair and set one directly before the door of the cell. He rested his cane against the wall and sat down. 'Maybe I can help you?' he said, slowly pulling off his leather gloves.

She looked at him suspiciously. 'Who are you?' she asked. 'Is that your carriage outside? Is that the one that takes those girls from the workhouse?'

The man seemed taken aback by her blunt question. He stared at her in surprise. Then he eyed her thoughtfully.

'Yes,' he said.

Although Cora had already known the answer, she was shocked to hear his reply. She felt a rising panic, and struggled to control it. She wouldn't go quietly this time. 'What did you do to them?' she asked, sizing up the distance to the door and wondering how many policemen might be in the station room above.

'They are all safe and well,' said the man. 'Happy, I think.'

Cora was confused. He smiled. 'I have an estate in the country, Cora, close to the sea. They are there, working for me – some in the dairy and the laundry, some in the house.'

Cora studied his face and for the first time she noticed

the kindness in his soft grey eyes. The man took off his hat and sat silently for a moment.

'My sister's child eloped with a scoundrel many years ago,' he said sadly. 'We discovered too late that she had lost her mind and died in that workhouse. I blame myself for not searching hard enough for her. Now, I do what I can to help some of those who have no other place to go.'

'But why do you do it in secret?'

'You may not know me, Cora Parry, but I am a public figure. This is my private business. There is no need for the world to know what I do. I prefer to visit the workhouse discreetly at night, when my carriage goes unnoticed and most of the inmates and staff are asleep. If word got out I would have all manner of poor women at my door and, sadly, I could never help them all. '

At that moment there were footsteps on the stairs and a brisk knock at the door. Sergeant Horner marched in carrying a sack. Cora recognised it at once.

'There's been a mistake, Sir,' he said, looking embarrassed and out of sorts. 'This is the wrong girl.'

'How could there be a mistake?' said the man. 'Bagwell caught her himself last night.'

'It's most peculiar, Sir,' said Sergeant Horner, 'but it's a genuine mistake all right.' Out of the sack he produced the stolen candlestick. Cora thought back. She remembered taking it with her when she ran from the house, but not having it on the bridge. She must have dropped it.

'One of my men saw another girl this morning on the very same bridge – same clothes, most unusual coincidence, Sir, except this one had the stolen article in her hand.'

'Where is she?' asked the man.

'That's the strangest thing of all, Sir,' said the Sergeant. 'Before he could approach her, the girl dropped the candlestick and jumped off the bridge into the river, right there in front of him – but there wasn't a splash! Not a sound. He looked everywhere, but she'd vanished! All he found was this.' He opened his hand and a tiny pearl button fell to the floor and rolled towards the cell. Cora reached through the bars and picked it up.

Her heart quickened. Carrie. She'd been given another chance. Sergeant Horner unlocked the cell and let her out.

'Sorry, Miss. It was a strange coincidence, but no harm done, I hope. You're free to go home now.'

The man offered his hand to Cora as she stepped out of the cell. 'Where will you go?' he asked. Cora had no answer. She was free, that was all she knew.

'Do you have work and friends?'

'No, Sir,' she said. She'd lost Joe's friendship for good now, and she knew she would never return to Farthing Court. 'But I can read and write.'

He smiled. 'We need help at our school in the village, Cora. There's a room at the schoolmistress's cottage if you'd like it.'

Cora beamed. Could it be true? She saw a white dress lying on a bed in a room flooded with sunshine.

'Oh, yes, Sir. I'd like that very much.'

At last, she could be who she wanted to be. She was going to live.

❧ 34 ❧

As Joe reached Salt Lane police station he didn't notice the carriage that was parked outside pull away.

It was left to Sergeant Horner to tell Joe the strange story of the girl in the red dress, the stolen candlestick and the vanishing thief.

So there really *had* been two girls, just as Carrie had told him all along, thought Joe as he walked home. That would explain the girl with the hatbox outside his window too. He wished he hadn't been so quick to accuse her. Joe hadn't completely understood the policeman's story, but all that mattered was that his friend was innocent and free. He'd probably never find out who took Pip that night, but there was no harm done after all, he told himself, and with a better lock on the door, maybe it was best forgotten.

Later that afternoon, to Joe's surprise, Cora came into the shop. Joe was busy taking in a bag of carpenter's tools which had to be written up in the pledge book item by item, so he couldn't go to her at once. Cora loitered, examining things on the shelf, thinking about the plans she had now made, and imagining how surprised Nellie was going to be when Cora's new friend rescued her from Walston, after hearing Cora tell her story. Joe watched her out of the corner of his eye. He'd never seen her look so happy.

'I came to find you,' he said at last, when the carpenter had left and all the tools had been put away. 'The policeman said it was all a mistake and you'd gone away.'

'Oh, Joe!' Cora didn't know where to start. 'There is so much to tell. I am going away, but it's a new start for me, a new life.'

'I've got things to tell, too,' said Joe excitedly. 'Everything's all right now – Pa and the shop and everything!' As they both began to talk at once, Pip came scampering in.

'Pip!' cried Cora. 'You're all right!'

Pip hurtled himself into her arms. Whatever he'd thought of their strange night-time adventure, he was as pleased to see her as ever.

'I'm sorry I didn't believe you,' said Joe.

'There are things you have to know,' she said. 'We must never have secrets again. My name, it's not really Carrie, it's Cora. Cora Parry.'

'What happened to Carrie?'

'She's gone now. For ever.'

Joe looked at her. The haunted look he'd often seen was

gone, as was the shadow in her eyes, the tension in her face. If that was Carrie, I like Cora better, he thought. Now wasn't the right time to tell her Rose's story. It could wait.

'I lost my senses, Joe,' she said. 'And I nearly lost you too.'

'Well, that won't happen again,' said Joe.

'Promise?'

'Promise!'

She hugged him tight.

At that moment Mr Tally arrived with Rose on his arm. 'You're just in time to give us an opinion on a fine cherry cake,' he said with a wink and that was the end of any serious talk for the rest of the afternoon.

When it was eventually time to go, Rose promised to continue Joe's lessons so that he could write to Cora.

'Let's not say goodbye then, Joe,' Cora said. 'I'll send a letter with my address and then you can reply. Write and tell me all about the wedding and Pip. There'll be lots of stories to tell, real stories this time.'

Joe nodded happily. 'Remember, Pip and me like sea stories best. But wait a minute.' He ran to the store-room and returned with Cora's box. 'You'll want to take this with you. And here's something to remind you of us.' He took the navy medal out of his pocket and slipped it inside.

Cora hesitated for a moment. Her mother's box had once meant so much to her, but maybe some things would always remain a mystery. She no longer needed to look for herself in the past. She took the box from Joe. Then she remembered the tiny pearl button in her pocket, and put that in too. Cora closed the lid. The past was precious but it was done. 'From now on it will be my treasure box, Joe.'

Cora tucked the box under her arm and stepped out into the street. She pictured herself placing it on a table beside a jug of primroses, in a room bathed in sea-bright light. She smiled.

A new story was waiting to begin. A real story that would belong to Cora Parry. Her own true adventure at last.